MURDER IN THE MAZE
The village of Redingote anticipated the usual misbehavior during the annual summer fête. But no one expected murder . . .

FROZEN STIFF
The new management consultant at Tesbury's grocery chain has annoyed a lot of people with his meddling. Now he's made someone angry enough to commit murder . . .

CORPSE IN THE KITCHEN
She was baking bread—until an unknown party turned the staff of life into the stuff of death . . . and choked her with a wad of raw dough. Now the heat is on Trewley and Stone . . .

DYING BREATH
Dr. Holbrook was a brilliant scientist—until somebody made him the guinea pig for an experiment in murder . . .

SEW EASY TO KILL
When a sabotaged sewing machine kills a student, Trewley and Stone have to find a murderer cut from an entirely different cloth than anyone ever suspected . . .

MORE MYSTERIES FROM THE
BERKLEY PUBLISHING GROUP . . .

MELISSA CRAIG MYSTERIES: She writes mystery novels—and investigates crimes when life mirrors art. "Splendidly lively." —*Publishing News*

by Betty Rowlands

A LITTLE GENTLE SLEUTHING	EXHAUSTIVE ENQUIRIES
OVER THE EDGE	MALICE POETIC
FINISHING TOUCH	

TREWLEY AND STONE MYSTERIES: Even the coziest English villages have criminal secrets . . . but fortunately, they also have Detectives Trewley and Stone to dig them up!

by Sarah J. Mason

MURDER IN THE MAZE	DYING BREATH
FROZEN STIFF	SEW EASY TO KILL
CORPSE IN THE KITCHEN	SEEING IS DECEIVING

INSPECTOR KENWORTHY MYSTERIES: Scotland Yard's consummate master of investigation lets no one get away with murder. "In the best tradition of British detective fiction!" —*Boston Globe*

by John Buxton Hilton

HANGMAN'S TIDE	TWICE DEAD
FATAL CURTAIN	RANSOM GAME
PLAYGROUND OF DEATH	FOCUS ON CRIME
CRADLE OF CRIME	CORRIDORS OF GUILT
HOLIDAY FOR MURDER	DEAD MAN'S PATH
LESSON IN MURDER	DEATH IN MIDWINTER
TARGET OF SUSPICION	

THE INSPECTOR AND MRS. JEFFRIES: He's with Scotland Yard. She's his housekeeper. Sometimes, her job can be murder . . .

by Emily Brightwell

THE INSPECTOR AND MRS. JEFFRIES	THE GHOST AND MRS. JEFFRIES
MRS. JEFFRIES DUSTS FOR CLUES	MRS. JEFFRIES TAKES STOCK
MRS. JEFFRIES ON THE BALL	MRS. JEFFRIES ON THE TRAIL
MRS. JEFFRIES PLAYS THE COOK	MRS. JEFFRIES AND THE MISSING ALIBI
MRS. JEFFRIES STANDS CORRECTED	MRS. JEFFRIES TAKES THE STAGE

CASSANDRA SWANN BRIDGE MYSTERIES: Cassie Swann is an expert at bridge. And her strategic skills are well suited to solving crimes as well . . . "A welcome new heroine." —*Publishers Weekly*

by Susan Moody

DEATH TAKES A HAND	GRAND SLAM
KING OF HEARTS	

SCOTLAND YARD MYSTERIES: Featuring Detective Superintendent Duncan Kincaid and his partner, Sergeant Gemma James . . . "Charming!"
—*New York Times Book Review*

by Deborah Crombie

A SHARE IN DEATH	ALL SHALL BE WELL
LEAVE THE GROVE GREEN	MOURN NOT YOUR DEAD

SEEING
IS
DECEIVING

Sarah J. Mason

BERKLEY PRIME CRIME, NEW YORK

SEEING IS DECEIVING

A Berkley Prime Crime Book / published by arrangement with the author

PRINTING HISTORY
Berkley Prime Crime edition / June 1997

The Putnam Berkley World Wide Web site address is
http://www.berkley.com

ISBN: 0-425-15901-9

Berkley Prime Crime Books are published by
The Berkley Publishing Group,
200 Madison Avenue, New York, NY 10016.
The name BERKLEY PRIME CRIME and the BERKLEY PRIME CRIME
design are trademarks belonging to Berkley Publishing Corporation.

PRINTED IN THE UNITED STATES OF AMERICA

10 9 8 7 6 5 4 3 2 1

One

"Aha!" A COMPLACENT fist smacked hard on a cardboard folder. "I thought so!"

Startled as much by the bang as by the exclamation, Detective Sergeant Stone looked across from her desk to that of her superior. The corrugated features of Detective Superintendent Trewley—the Plainclothes Prune, as he was called by officers safely out of earshot—looked back at her. The normally mournful bloodhound face was creased by a ferocious grin.

"I *knew* you'd sleep badly last night." The bloodhound continued to grin. Or did he more closely resemble a bulldog? The definitive decision had never been made, though not for want of trying on the part of Trewley's colleagues. "Nightmares, I told myself." The bloodhound rolled his eyes. "Sleepwalking, even," he crowed. "I had a little bet with the wife I'd catch you out in a yawn before you'd been in the place five minutes and I was right."

Stone glanced at her wristwatch, always more accurate than the clock on the office wall. "Ten minutes, I think," she amended gently. "Credit where credit is due, please." Her accents were those of a weary martyr. "And *I'll* bet Mrs. Trewley was at least sympathetic to my problem—which is more than you seem to be, sir."

"Umph. Yes, she was." The bloodhound grinned with even greater ferocity. "But it doesn't stop me winning, mind." He sighed. "If she'll let me," he added glumly.

Now it was Stone's turn to grin. "Your wife has put you on another diet," she cheerfully deduced. "And you've just won a stay of execution?" She ignored the superintendent's wince. "I call it pretty mean of you to take advantage of my—of our—misfortunes like that."

"Then you should've told Young What's-His-Name to sleep in the spare room," growled Trewley. For whimsical reasons of his own, he never referred in any other fashion to the traffic officer with whom Stone shared her private life. "I can't have you yawning your head off all day just because *he's* upset about these television people." The superintendent removed his spectacles to wag them at his sergeant in reproof. "Now if you had only got your degree, my girl, you could have prescribed sleeping pills for the pair of you last night. And then there would've been a decent day's work done around here by more than just me."

"If," Stone reminded him, "I *had* graduated from medical school, I wouldn't be working here at all. Think what you'd have missed then."

"Umph." She had a point. Although he would never tell her so for fear of swelling her sleek dark head, Trewley considered his lively young sergeant a decided asset to the Allshire force, and believed that Stone accepted his good opinion as her due. Having studied for some years to be a doctor, she had abandoned that particular form of public service when her inability to tolerate the sight of blood became acute. Medicine's loss was Allingham's—and the superintendent's—gain.

Trewley had been wary at first of her lengthy education, but he had been impressed by her black belt in judo and her quick wits. The day he admitted that his advancing years required the use of reading glasses had set the final seal of approval on the working relationship of this theoretically uneven detective partnership.

"Caffeine," said Trewley. "Talking of prescribing things, I may not be a professional like some, but I'd say that's what you need to wake you up."

"It was only one yawn!" Stone pushed back her chair and rose to her feet. "Still, I can take a hint as well as anyone,

I suppose." Again she grinned at him. "Another supposition on my part being that you want some coffee, too, sir. Black," she added, in deference to the absent Mrs. Trewley. "Without," she added further, as Trewley grimaced.

Then he snorted. "Yes, I might have known you'd side with her," he said and sighed. "Look," he went on, "I can just about put up with being nagged at home"—as well as a loving wife, the superintendent had three teenage daughters—"but I can do with a break from it at work. I'll have tea, thanks—good and strong, mind, to make up for the rest of it." After his heroic concession, lugubrious brown bloodhound eyes met dancing hazel ones in a conspiratorial plea. "Be a good girl and bring me an iced bun, and I'll stand you a pint at lunch."

Stone hesitated. She knew how much her superior's spouse worried about his weight and his blood pressure. The former medic thought there was some justification for those worries, but there was also some overreaction. "A plain bun," she said firmly, "and you're on. And I'll have the same." This was another heroic concession, for Stone had been blessed with a fast-burning metabolism that allowed her to eat more or less what she liked without putting on an ounce. She was particularly fond of iced buns, but she was also fond of her superior. It didn't seem fair to torment him by eating forbidden food right under his nose.

Trewley chuckled. "It's woken you up, that's one thing. He'll have kept you awake half the night directing traffic in his sleep, I shouldn't wonder." Then he sighed again. "But what the devil possessed them to make their blasted film on market day of all days?"

"Realism," said Stone. "Or so they said in that letter, if you remember. Spontaneous authenticity."

"Authenticity be damned," snarled Trewley, stopping himself just in time from saying something else. He remembered the letter very well, but a new diet always brought out the worst in his nature.

"Come on, sir, look on the bright side. At least they told us what they were planning. Can you imagine what it would have been like if they'd just arrived out of the blue and started getting under everyone's feet without so much as a by-your-leave?"

"Oh, I can imagine." Once more Trewley produced the wolfish grin. "The same way Young What's-His-Name can— But you're right, let's look on the bright side. If he's the sort that photographs well, the lad could end up a star. Even if they *had* had advance warning to rehearse their patter and to dress fancy, those stallholders wouldn't stand a chance. Eat your heart out, James Bond. Here comes Traffic Man in his customised panda car, doing handbrake turns around the organic veg. and the wicker baskets and the cut-price videos off the back of an unmarked lorry . . ."

Stone shook her head in reproof for his careless slander. "We've never managed to prove anything directly, sir."

"But we can hazard a pretty good guess." Another chuckle rumbled deep in the bulldog's throat. "How d'you reckon they'd care to film a spontaneously authentic arrest? Life as it's really lived in an English market town in the late twentieth century. I'll pass the word, if you like. Bring that video bloke in on suspicion again—he's an old hand at the game by now. I daresay he won't mind adding a spot of local colour for the sake of stardom, and the action'll give our lot a chance to show their paces."

"Yes, sir. Very droll." Stone prepared to vanish in pursuit of tea and buns. "But there's the risk we could end up with rather too much, um, action. Something gives me the idea the chief constable wouldn't thank us if the Massacre of Allingham Market appeared on prime-time television. You know as well as I do how those stallholders stick together— and if we warn all of them it's just a put-up job, what price spontaneity then?"

He chuckled again as she opened the door. "Don't give up the day job, Trewley. Is that what you're saying?"

"Let's put it this way, sir. I should think they'd feel happier with Cecil B. DeMille working on their film—and he's been dead for almost forty years."

She was halfway to the canteen by the time he understood the full import of her remark. "Cheeky young madam," he muttered, then sighed as he replaced the spectacles on his nose and settled to his paperwork again.

DIOGENES IS SAID to have taken his lantern to look for an honest man. Had the philosopher used it to illuminate Allingham Market in such a search, it must have shone so brightly that the backlights and other technical tricks employed by the three-man video crew would have been rendered unnecessary on this overcast spring day. Trewley had been not so much cynical as realistic in his assessment of the moral character of those who manned the stalls and cried the various wares on sale to (let us hope) a more virtuous populace than themselves.

"Oy!" A giant of a man with rolled-up sleeves showing arms tattooed from wrist to elbow glared at the nearest camera. "Watcher think yer playing at? Who gave you the right to go taking pictures of folk without asking?" He did not speak in the superstitious accents of one who believes that in the taking of his picture a piece of his immortal soul is also being taken.

"Sorry," said the picture-taker at once. "It's only a background shot for a television documentary on English Market Towns. May I just have a few feet of you, and your customers?" he added, as a tall, pale, elderly man with gold-rimmed glasses who had been trying to buy three pounds of tomatoes turned to blink in surprise at the cause of this disturbance.

"Television," said the tattooed belligerent, folding his arms. Those with keen eyesight might have observed how the mermaid on his left arm thus became somewhat lewdly involved with the sea serpent on his right. "Ah, now. Well, that's different. Thought you might be snoops from the gover'ment trying to catch me out, see. I never thought of the telly. Why dincher say so straight off?"

"Sorry," said the picture-taker again. "I was trying to be . . . unobtrusive. If you'd known I was here filming, it might have made you self-conscious. Less . . . natural. If we'd wanted actors, we would have brought them with us."

"You don't want a loader bleeding cream puffs, you want

real people," translated the devotee of aquatic acrobatics. "Well, we don't mind helping yer aht with yer documentary if it's real people yer after . . . Eh, Mr. Paine?"

"Er," said the man with the gold rims, blinking again. He still wanted his tomatoes and was now faced with a dilemma as getting-back-to-work squared up to courtesy . . . and won. "Yes," said Mr. Paine. "I'm afraid I do. Mind, that is, if it's going to take long, which I fear it may. I, er, don't care, you know, to stay away from the shop for too long." He nodded politely to the face behind the viewfinder. "I'm sure you know your job, but these things are never as quick as one hopes they will be, are they? If you wouldn't mind waiting until someone in less of a hurry than I am comes along, I should, er, be greatly obliged to you."

"Okay by me," said the face cheerily. "But I'll use you as a dummy run, if that's all right."

"Yer want the full business?" enquired the tattooed one, as Mr. Paine prepared to put in his request a second time. The face signalled an affirmative. The tattooed one took a deep breath. "Luvverly toms, fresh today!" he roared, the veins in his mighty neck swelling with the effort. "Getcher mushrooms here, girls, picked this morning just for you! The carrots is so good the rabbits was coming to the field by bus with their little spades to dig 'em aht before I got there . . ."

This highly persuasive barking had such an effect on Mr. Paine that he added mushrooms (to which he was indifferent) and carrots (which gave him indigestion if not thoroughly cooked) to his shopping list, though he drew the line at celery so crisp some folk had to wear earplugs to eat it. The camcorder whined faintly in the background as the transaction was completed. Mr. Paine headed thankfully back to the optician's where, as manager, he was more in control of his surroundings, yielding his chance for stardom to a pair of elderly sisters clad in matching hand-knitted cardigans, who trotted up carrying string bags already bulging with balls and cones of cut-price yarn wrapped in cellophane that squeaked rhythmically as bag bumped against bag with every step.

A long, lean, grey-faced man had been an interested spectator of the market square proceedings. In a worn tweed jacket with frayed leather edging on the cuffs and leather patches on the elbows, and with a glowing cigarette hanging from the corner of his mouth, E. M. "no relation" Forster, one-time Fleet Street hopeful, now faded demon reporter of the *Allingham Argus*, ambled up and down the rows of stalls in the wakes of the various camcorder operators, watching the reactions of traders and shoppers as they were filmed for media posterity, and making trenchant remarks into a pocket tape recorder.

"Press," said Forster, when politely challenged by a young man who had to be the leader of the video team. Only one in complete control of himself and his world would have the nerve to wear, in a county town on market day, a needlecord two-piece in shades of rust with flared trousers and a pink polka-dot cravat.

"Damn," said Rusty Flares. "We really wanted to keep this quiet. How the hell did you know we were coming?" Too late he noticed that Forster was holding the tape recorder where his voice was bound to be heard. "Now look here," Rusty began.

"I'm looking," said Forster equably. "Listening, too," he added as Rusty Flares said nothing more.

After a moment's cogitation the younger man decided to play the all-chums-together card. "Look, you won't queer our pitch, will you?" he began. "You know how it is with this sort of job. We're making a fly-on-the-wall documentary on the English Market Town—we want authentic spontaneity, you know the sort of thing—and Allingham's only the first of the places we mean to film. The trouble is, once people know we're likely to turn up, they can't help it—they become . . . artificial, less real. Less relaxed," he amended with a wary eye on the tape recorder. "Couldn't you keep your feature back until after we've finished filming everywhere? Then—well, the more publicity we can get, the better." He gestured expansively. "Funding. Sponsorship. *You* know."

"When?" enquired E. M. Forster.

He was answered by a devastating smile and the suggestion that, weather permitting, a fortnight should be about right. Forster nodded. "Suits me," he said. "The *Argus* only comes out once a week." The smile wavered. Forster shrugged. "Takes me that long to work my stuff up into anything I think might be worth reading, without photographs." He held out a hand and demonstrated its shakiness. "Swap you for a few decent stills, and you're on."

Rusty Flares had to settle this. "D'you mean you're . . . *local*? Not from one of the nationals?"

"Never said I was."

Rusty Flares let out an exasperated sigh. "No, but . . ."

E. M. Forster looked at him. "Easy mistake to make," he said kindly. "I'm . . . good. Fleet Street anytime I want it, but I like it here. It's my patch. Not much I can't find out if I take the trouble. The only one who knew you were coming—"

"Yes," broke in the Rusty one indignantly. "How *did* you know?"

"I'm good," reiterated Forster. "Surprise you how much I can find out," he enlarged as Rusty stifled a sigh, "if I want to. Sources," he concluded, waving the tape recorder in a wild sweep that almost took off Rusty's startled nose.

"Oh," said Rusty Flares as Forster fell silent, gazing with sudden interest over his shoulder. "Oh, well." There was no response beyond a lopsided grin and a ripple of tweed as Forster inhaled, coughed bronchitically—the cigarette somehow stayed where it had been—and inhaled a second time as he prepared to move away. "Oh, well," said Rusty Flares again, acknowledging defeat as the older man gave him a quizzical look, set himself in lazy motion, and ambled past him with a valedictory nod.

"Er—thanks," Rusty found himself saying to the tweeded back before it was engulfed in a crowd of shoppers. The Cardigan Sisters had just finished haggling with a stall holder over the price of a wicker basket, the whole exchange having been immortalised by one of the two junior members of the video team. E. M. Forster lengthened his stride and caught up with the chattering, still-indignant Cardigans. He introduced himself, pinched out his cigarette and popped it behind his ear, switched on the recorder, and started to ask his questions.

Questions—and answers—were not as clear on the first attempt as they might have been in less noisy surroundings. Allingham Market was a busy place. Rows of stalls criss-crossed the square in theoretically neat ranks; lorries and vans unloaded top-up stock and caused jams to break a traffic warden's heart as drivers of obstructed cars cursed and hooted, and the delivery men cursed back. Pedestrians tripped over unexpected cardboard boxes tumbling, crushed and discarded, from careless heaps into the path of the unwary so that further cries and curses filled the air.

"Authenticity," muttered E. M. Forster as he surveyed with a jaded eye the scene from the top of the town hall steps. For the moment his interviews were on hold, and he had retired out of interruption range to put a welcome match to the tip of his half-smoked cigarette. The pale March sun had at last broken through a creamy cloud cover to glisten weakly on plastic canopies and shoppers' glasses and the inquisitive lenses of the three video cameras weaving their spontaneous way around the serried stalls. Traders with midriff bulges from the money bags on their low-slung belts dragged coins from their denim depths and chaffed customers offering notes about the likelihood of forgery. When the weight of change promised discomfort, neighbourly eyes kept watch on stalls while bags were taken to the nearby branch of the Allshire and National Bank to have their contents counted into safekeeping.

"Fly on the wall." Forster exhaled a stream of smoke in the direction of a bluebottle that had buzzed too close. It did a hurried reverse somersault and beat a wide retreat. "Realism," said Forster, watching a waddling masculine rear pause halfway up the steps of the bank for breath. He sighed and closed his eyes to enjoy the rest of his cigarette in peace.

The shotgun blast destroyed that peace completely.

Two

WITH THE PASSAGE of time and the arrival of technology, the security arrangements of Britain's high-street banks have undergone considerable change. The genteel era of seasoned oak, polished brass, and ledgers kept by hand has long since passed. The open counter with its trusting lack of privacy has been replaced by the bulletproof plate-glass wall with its malevolent pigeonholes. Through those pigeonholes clerks peer from their fortress, attempting to pass the time of day with customers recognised not by name but by account number and by the facility with which they pitch their voices to overcome the muffled interference of the never-quite-in-working-order microphones installed by some warped ergonomic genius in the exact spot where the majority of customers find it most convenient to spread their assorted paperwork as they wrestle with the financial conundrums of the late twentieth century.

Banks with a desire to be user-friendly have of late been inclined towards modest counterrevolution. Many feet of plate glass have accordingly been removed and, in the Green spirit of the age, recycled as table- or desktops or display shelves in upmarket emporia owned by interior decorators of a modernistic bent. While enough glass remains in situ for clerks who actually handle the cash to be confident of their personal safety, financial advisers, however, whose sympathies lie more with rows of abstract numbers manoeuvred around a screen, rather than the physi-

cal coin of the realm, sit well outside the pigeonholed
fortress, facing their customers with only the width of a desk
between them.

This practice ensures that when masked and violent men
burst through a bank's main door brandishing weapons, it is
the financial advisers, together with those they are advising
and any customers queueing for their turn at the plate-glass
wall, who are at the greatest risk of being shot.

"All right—hands up! Nobody move!"

Three figures had erupted through the main door into the
carpeted hush of the Allshire and National Bank. All three
thugs carried shotguns—barrels sawn off for lethal effect.
All three wore unisex jeans and baggy tracksuit tops. All
three had stockings over their heads, squashing their features into nightmarish, out-of-focus deformities so that not
even their closest acquaintances would have known them.
As the leading thug screamed his orders, he made a scornful
gesture at the red light of a watching security camera before
pointing his shotgun in the face of a terrified woman.

"One wrong move and she gets both barrels, see? You
two—get on with it!"

Using far more force than necessary, his companions
elbowed and buffeted their way through a silent and
frightened crowd who, as they passed, struggled to maintain
their balance lost for fear of being accused of movement.
The thugs sniggered at these struggles, and waved their guns
in an extravagant display of mastery. A child in its mother's
tightened arms began to cry. The inexorable stare of the
leading thug's shotgun slid for a moment from the terrified
woman to the crying child: The mother uttered a muted
shriek and slithered with buckling knees to the floor. On the
way down the child bumped its head and, after one shrill
scream, was silent.

"Leave it!" barked the leading thug, showing his teeth as
he brought the shotgun's hollow gaze to focus again on its
original target. The terrified woman read destruction in the
bleak twin depths and, already white, turned whiter, letting
out in a gurgle the breath she had long held without
knowing she did so. The leader laughed.

"Get on with it, I said!"

The taller of the two secondary figures thus addressed now rapped on the door dividing the public from the business area. His associate, again with unnecessary force, thrust an elderly woman out of her place in front of the plate glass; cracked a vindictive shotgun barrel against the glass to draw attention already won; jabbed a sinister, gloved finger at a pale, redheaded youth who sat frozen on his chair; and then jerked a contemptuous thumb in the direction of the door. Obeying both this command and the urgent mutterings of his superior, the redhead stumbled across to the door and with shaking hands opened it.

The taller gunman poked his shotgun into the ribs of the redheaded youth. Muscles visibly clenched under the baggy tracksuit top. The eyes of the redhead, greenish grey in his now grey-green face, went to the trigger. The boy grunted as the shotgun stabbed his midriff. "Cash," said the man behind the trigger. "Quick."

His smaller companion, after a quick look towards where the leader of the gang held a room full of people paralysed for the sake of the terrified woman, slipped past the taller second thug into the inner area and kept watch as the redheaded youth went on unsteady legs from the door to the safe, which his superior was opening in response to a meaningful twitch of the second thug's expressive thumb. Nylon holdalls appeared from tracksuit pockets and were spread open on the floor. Bundles of notes—a wordless growl from the smaller thug rejected the cash—were dropped hurriedly into the gaping zip-fastener gullets until a signal from the leading thug outside called a halt to this financial feeding frenzy.

"Nobody move," warned the taller of the two within the business area. The redheaded youth gave a sigh and fainted. The taller gunmen kicked him in the ribs as he and his silent companion grabbed the holdalls and hurried out.

The terrified woman turned from white to sickly grey. "Please . . ." she began.

"Shut it!" The leading thug swung his shotgun up and

round to strike her on the side of the head. Metal cracked horribly on bone. The woman collapsed.

In their hurry the junior thugs wasted no time on the petty buffets in which they had indulged only a few moments—or had it been a few hours?—earlier. Even the leader seemed more interested now in the bulging nylon holdalls than in keeping watch over captives who, with his immediate hostage out of danger, were starting to find their second wind. The market traders of Allshire are a hardy breed. They may be taken by surprise on rare occasions, but they are never surprised for long. Muscles, tuned over many years of humping merchandise in heavy crates, were quietly flexed. Weight was surreptitiously shifted from one foot to another for swift action when the opportunity might come.

The ladies of Allshire are likewise caught at a disadvantage for only a little while. The elderly woman thrust aside at the plate-glass wall tightened her grasp on her heavy shopping bag as she calculated distance and trajectory. The young mother who had fainted opened her eyes, saw her offspring silent on the floor with a bloody scalp, and prepared to do battle. Out of sight in the private area, a ripple of wary movement ran through those who had witnessed the looting of the safe. The panic button, pressed the instant someone had realized what was happening outside, was pressed again with greater vigour as people began to move.

"Nobody move," cautioned the leading thug as his cohorts joined him, passed him, and headed for the door with their weapons poised to gun down anyone unlucky enough to cross their path. Once there, the taller of the two whipped round to guard the apparently unmoving crowd while his leader made his own escape to the main door.

The door, covered only by the shorter thug, was pushed open by a man wearing horn-rimmed spectacles. The muzzle of the short thug's shotgun beckoned him in to stand against the wall. The bespectacled man uttered a gasp, but did as he was told.

At his gasp the other two gunmen turned as one: They turned back just too late. The elderly woman hurled her shopping bag. It fell short, but two market traders had unbuckled their money bags and, flailing them in forceful circles, now charged towards the three at the door. Other traders joined in. The young mother snatched her child out of the way of running feet and cheered them on.

The thugs, panicked, pulled their triggers as they ran. One wild shot severed a cord supporting an overhead display of interest rates. This collapsed sideways against a free-standing board praising the benefits of a regular savings account: It overbalanced into the chest of the man in the horn-rimmed spectacles and knocked him first sideways, then senseless as his head hit the wall. Two of the largest market traders, easy targets, slumped writhing to the ground. Only one of them was cursing as he writhed. The elderly woman, her burst of adrenaline exhausted, began to shiver. An elderly man with a military moustache picked up a telephone from the nearest desk—the financial adviser had gone into hysterics—and dialled nine-nine-nine.

The thugs were out, running down the steps of the Allshire and National Bank. Their leader turned to fire a shot at any from inside who might be tempted to follow, warning any from the market square who might be tempted to interfere that they should mind their own business.

E. M. Forster, on the steps of the town hall, opened his eyes and dropped his cigarette. His business was to watch, to listen, and to report. He saw running men in masks; he heard shouts and a gunned engine. In response to the leader's shot a car—anonymous dark blue or black, with its number plate obscured by splashes of mud—screeched around a corner into the square and came to a momentary halt outside the bank. Doors were flung open, the nylon holdalls were slung in, and the thugs scrambled in after them. Doors were slammed, and the car, with another vicious gunning of the engine, sped off in a cloud of blue exhaust mixed with the smell of burning rubber.

A middle-aged man brooding on his imminent redundancy crossed the road without due care and attention. The wing of the anonymous car clipped him on the thigh and hurled him backwards. He struck his head on the cobbled stones with which the town council had recently prettified the area of the market and its surroundings. Blood began to seep from the gash in his scalp.

The two-tone yodel of a siren was heard in the near distance, rapidly approaching. Blue flashing lights were reflected in nearby shop windows.

The police had arrived.

The events of the past few minutes had thrown an unexpected spanner into the video works. Shotguns and violence and high-speed flight added a sudden, new dimension to life in the late twentieth-century English Market Town. Once he had realised what was happening, the leader of the camcorder team hardly knew which way to warn his colleagues to look as shoppers exclaimed, traders agonised over whether to charge to the rescue of their fellows or to guard their takings, and truant schoolchildren yelled hysterical support for those who, like themselves, were on the wrong side of the law.

The video crew plunged headlong through the market crowd for a better view of the bank. They filmed the end of the thugs' rush down the granite steps, the shotgun signal, the screeching arrival of the getaway car, the loading into that car of loot and looters together, and, by no means last, the tyre-scorching handbrake turn that sent the car back in the direction from which it had come in the first place.

"No point chasing them," said the leader of the video team, nodding at the cloud of blue-black exhaust. "But if we play our cards right with the rest of it, we've got a scoop to end all scoops here. Prime-time television news, that's us!"

They continued to film. In the wake of two ambulances, more police cars arrived. Some swerved around clusters of too-curious bystanders drifting now into the road to chase after the fugitives; some disgorged uniformed officers who, dividing their duties, either sprinted up the steps to check inside the bank or began their traditional "Now then, now then, what's all this?" routine. While this worked reasonably well on the citizens of Allshire, it did not please the alien video team to move along as requested. Their leader cried freedom of information and the public's right to know: with the result that they were left, reluctantly, alone, once the warning had been given that copies of their film must be submitted to the police before anyone else could see them. The leader muttered darkly of censorship, but was induced to agree once Detective Superintendent Trewley, more grim-faced than usual because Stone had driven him to the scene, came and menaced him for a few minutes in his best bulldog manner.

E. M. Forster stamped out his cigarette where it lay on the town hall steps, sending up a forlorn spiral of smoke. He fumbled in his pockets, inserted a blank tape into his recorder, and descended from the marble heights to approach the first of his eyewitnesses. For once he was spoiled for a choice. He only hoped they wouldn't all speak at the same time: He was good, but not that good. He'd better remind the young whippersnapper in charge of the video crew that they had a gentlemen's agreement in the matter of stills. Superintendent Trewley's little exchange with the youngster hadn't gone unnoticed by "Nothing Gets Past Me" Forster, who could hazard a guess as to what the bloodhound wanted. Well, the police would have access to the bank's closed-circuit shots as well as to the video footage. They shouldn't begrudge a jaded hack his first chance for a five-star scoop in months—if not years.

MUCH HAS BEEN written of the singular fact that around every crisis, great or small, life goes on as usual. People in the eye of the hurricane find it incredible that those on its outer fringes may notice no more of its passage than that there is an unaccustomed fluttering of leaves on the topmost branches of some of the tallest trees. Not every member of the local constabulary was engaged with the aftermath of the Allshire and National Bank robbery.

And even some of those who were did not realise the fact until too late.

The traffic officer with whom Detective Stone shared her private life had over the years become resigned to the selfishness of drivers, the recklessness of cyclists, and the thoughtlessness of pedestrians in the matter of the Highway

Code. This dismal triad was, however, as nothing to the cussedness of the British workman, who has honed to perfection the art of maximum confusion caused with the minimum of personal effort.

It is widely held among traffic departments and town councils that there is at some hidden locality a training school for the Ancient and Honourable Guild of Navvies, a brotherhood whose existence can be deduced from the very strongest of circumstantial evidence. This dedicated band, it is said, swears fraternal allegiance on a copper tea urn, and offers midnight sacrifice on the drum of a stalled steam-roller; its badge is two crossed pickaxes surmounted by a fluorescent Stop sign. Members of the Guild are bound by the most fearsome oaths to read the gazetteers to find the busiest day of the week in their target town, and to study the latest maps—incorporating the most recent one-way-street systems and diversions—to ensure that they pick the most disruptive of the victim's streets in which to dig their holes in the exact middle of the asphalt ribbon. In order to qualify for higher status among their peers, they learn how to offset the timers on temporary traffic lights so that the green signal at one end overlaps the red at the other by the correct number of extra seconds in proportion to the distance between them.

It was a group of graduates in this final art who were now exercising the patience of the life's companion of Detective Sergeant Stone. The gas main under Allingham's busiest crossroads having sprung a slow leak, warnings had been posted through letter boxes for several hundred yards in all directions that nobody should strike a match or close a window until things had been put right. Passing pedestrians with lighted pipes or cigarettes in their mouths were advised to take a different route if they didn't want to become Home Office (Accidents, Non-Domestic) statistics. The Highways Department sent a man to disconnect the crossroads traffic lights. The Navvies of the Gas Board rubbed their horny hands and prepared to set joyfully to work . . .

"That angle is rather sharp," observed the soulmate of Detective Sergeant Stone to the leader of the Gas Board gang. He pointed sternly from the red Stop sign on the verge beside the temporary lights to the accompanying row of plastic cones redirecting traffic from the wrong side of the road to the right. "If a long vehicle coming the other way misjudges the gap, it'll run smack into whatever is at the front of the queue waiting here. I'd like you to move the whole lot back another ten yards or so, please."

The gas man was too shrewd to make outright refusal. He sucked in his breath and frowned. "Move it back. Well, now," he said, and frowned again, shaking his head sadly and clicking his tongue before launching into a lengthy explanation he hoped would be too technical for the traffic man to refute.

Hope was in vain. Detective Sergeant Stone was not the only university-educated member of the Allingham force, and for a BA in Civil Engineering, making mincemeat of the gas man's argument was a matter of moments only. Bested, the man beat a sullen retreat to stand scowling on the verge as the Stop sign and lights were shuffled a grudging twenty feet farther from the plastic cones. Seeing the compromise accepted by Stone's Young What's-His-Name with a cheery nod of encouragement made the gas man scowl all the more. He caught the eye of his henchmen and made a cabbalistic sign, instantly comprehensible by any of the Brotherhood.

"You want to check the other end as well?" The henchman jerked his thumb towards the second set of lights on their flimsy tripod. The faulty green Go bulb had been chosen with care, and the shortening of one tripod leg to make an overbalance inevitable should the apparatus be clipped by a passing car was a masterpiece of fine measurement.

Young What's-His-Name gazed up the road. "I checked it earlier, thanks," he said. "It still seems okay from where I'm standing."

"Yes, well, appearances can be deceptive," returned the henchman with a wink for his superior. "We've had to move it a bit, see? Better safe than sorry, that's our motto." He made his own cabbalistic sign, invisible to his uniformed companion. On the nearby grass verge, the gas man grinned. As the other two walked away, he bent to fiddle dexterously with two short lengths of wire at the rear underside of the temporary lights, and was upright and at ease by the time the two had walked back again.

"All systems go, then," said Young What's-His-Name.

"All systems go," echoed the gas man equably.

Some were to go with rather more energy than anyone could have rightly expected.

——————— Three ———————

THE HEALTH AND Safety people have poked their regulatory noses into a great many aspects of life in late twentieth-century Britain. Sometimes the resultant legislation, seen as unwarranted interference by the Nanny State, is ignored; sometimes it is seen as no more than common sense made law at last, and willingly accepted. The compulsory wearing of heavy-duty earmuffs for those using noisy machinery is a case in point. Nobody in his right mind—the macho culture of the British workman notwithstanding—wants to risk a premature loss of hearing.

The Gas Board gang were entirely in their right mind as the hardened steel teeth of their pneumatic drills chewed and gnawed and roared at the thickly layered asphalt and concrete and rubble of the Allingham crossroads. With his ears dutifully muffled, no Guild member could have been expected to hear the frantic hoots and shouts of drivers who, trying to navigate the narrow space between stout kerb-stones on one side and plastic cones—a flimsy protection from the fearsome chaos of excavation—on the other, met an oncoming vehicle in the middle of what they had trustingly believed to be their road. The leader of the navvies had done his job well. The temporary traffic lights flicked their mischievous signal from red to green, from green to red, with a malignantly mistimed cunning. It did not happen in an instant—suspicion must not be aroused—

but within fifteen minutes of a slowly-closing overlap the lights at both ends suddenly worked as one.

Vehicles moving off upon the simultaneous Go lost their nerve in desperate unison as the right-of-way was claimed in both directions. As those behind cried "Forward!" so those behind, correctly interpreting the hasty red gleam of brake lights and the urgent white fire of reverse, cried "Back!" A timid individual who had passed his test only three weeks earlier struck, in his obedient panic, the front bumper of the vehicle behind. This car, an Austin, crashed back into the bonnet of a Citroen, which slewed sideways and hit the kerb to rebound against the nearside wing of a blue Toyota. The Toyota lurched into the radiator of a Peugeot . . .

The gas man and his comrades beamed as the results of the timid one's panic dominoed to the very end of the queue, where an aged Ford pickup full of building supplies mounted the kerb and shed half its load in the path of a lorry rumbling to a halt beside the treacherous traffic light, which now showed innocent red. Some lengths of copper pipe rolled off, bounced up, and clanged against the lorry's bonnet before falling under its heavy wheels. All save one of the pipes were squashed into submission: But one was more than enough. Avoiding every wheel with diabolic agility, it bounced up again to become entangled in some vital part of the lorry's workings . . .

With a tortured scream, the lorry's engine died. Inside the cab, the dashboard lights went out.

Under the bonnet, a single spark gave life to the flow of petrol from a severed duct . . .

"Look out!" roared the driver, hurling himself through the door almost before he'd opened it. "She's going to go!"

As bystanders gaped, go she did, in a sudden scorching flurry of flame that spread from front to rear number plates in seconds. The air was filled with boiling clouds of smoke made thick and pungent as the contents of the lorry caught fire. The bystanders began to cough and choke.

The lorry driver, closest of all to the conflagration, staggered to a convenient lamppost and leaned weakly against it, mopping his brow and cursing to himself. Above the spluttering cries of the bystanders and the roaring of the fire, his bewildered ears heard the sound of running feet. "Are you all right?" an unknown voice demanded. The driver gazed blankly at the breathless, white-faced young man wearing a police uniform who had materialised before him. "Was there anyone in there with you?" asked the young man, pointing to the burning lorry as the driver could only stare. "Is there anyone still inside?"

"Bananas," groaned the driver as he slumped farther down the lamppost.

"Is there? I've got to know," urged Young What's-His-Name, ignoring the slur. He knew that shock affected people in many different ways.

The driver groaned again. "Only bananas . . . Oh, blimey," he said with his hands over his eyes. "Omigawd, that's the biggest damn bloody banana fritter you'll ever see in your life . . ."

But Young What's-His-Name did not hear him. Reassured that no rescue attempt was necessary, he was using his personal radio to summon the fire brigade and a panda or two. It was everybody's bad luck that the blaze should have occurred on the far side of town away from the fire station—and, to make matters worse, on market day, when the roads both in and out of town were so much more congested. Those who said Traffic Division didn't have a clue what life was all about had it absolutely wrong, with bells on.

"Hey, you!" Young What's-His-Name beckoned to the leader of the navvies as the next in authority until help could arrive. The gas man, feeling slightly guilty over the unexpected success of his unorthodox wiring arrangements, came hurrying across to hear Young What's-His-Name's instructions.

"Get some of your men to move pedestrians away in case that thing blows sky-high. Tell anyone else they can't walk down here." Young What's-His-Name frowned. "I want all oncoming cars stopped, and the ones already queueing told to back up out of range—as if they haven't been trying hard enough already," he added grimly. Above the sound of flambéing bananas and choking bystanders the revving of engines in desperate reverse and the accompanying hoots of frantic horns were loud on the smoky air.

"We could move some of our diversion signs to send folk down a side road or two," suggested the gas man, surprised at how his conscience pricked him.

"Any of your crowd local? We don't want to make things worse by jamming traffic into a dead end and with no hope of turning around. All those residential streets tend to look the same if you don't know your way about."

"No problem," said the gas man, his chest swelling. He would square it with the Guild later. "There's Jim, he'll do for one, and—"

"Fine." The personal radio was tucked back inside the pocket. "Leave it to you, right?" The policeman's quick eye had observed the lorry driver's final collapse from a slumped to a supine position at the foot of the lamppost. It was the turn of the constabulary's conscience to prick. Shock-suffocation-heart attack—"I'd better see to him," said Young What's-His-Name, blessing both his first-aid training and the additional knowledge he had gleaned from his years of intimacy with Detective Sergeant Stone.

He dropped to his knees beside the driver. "Are you okay? Don't try to move. Can you hear me?" He strained to hear the reply.

Even as he strained he was deafened by an outburst of yelling and a sudden scream of brakes. Instinct had him leaping to his feet, the invalid's reply unheard as he looked down the road to where three navvies were running to shout with waving arms at a high-speed car—anonymous dark blue or black, its number plates obscured by smears of mud—that had appeared as if from nowhere and had evidently overtaken the backwards-crawling queue of vehicles with the idea of jumping the lights. The sight of the burning lorry must have come as a shock. As the navvies gesticulated and bystanders bawled and the traffic policeman could only stare, the anonymous car whipped round in a handbrake circle seldom bettered by an instructor on the force's training pan, and sped off with a screech of tyres down a distant side road.

And was lost to sight and hearing.

"Maniacs," muttered the driver of the burning lorry as he struggled to turn over and pull himself to his feet. "Omigawd—my head!" He collapsed in a coughing heap as Young What's-His-Name forgot the fleeing car and dropped to his knees again.

"Keep still," the traffic officer advised. The coughing became more insistent as the driver ignored this sage advice. The sage sighed. "Oh, well, if you must . . . Then lean against me, and I'll hold your head off the ground. The ambulance will be here before long."

So he hoped; and so it was. With it came a brace of fire engines, followed almost at once by a crackle on the personal radio.

"All points bulletin," said the voice that spoke as the crackle faded. "Armed robbery at the Allingham branch of the Allshire and National Bank. Suspect vehicle a dark blue or black saloon, last seen heading out of town in a northerly direction towards the ring-road intersection with the High Street . . ."

For a moment, Young What's-His-Name was lost for words. He looked at the lorry driver, now being tended by a gaggle of white coats with oxygen and stethoscopes and similar equipment . . .

"Omigawd," he said.

His tape wasn't yet full, but his batteries had gone flat. E. M. Forster shrugged philosophically, lit another cigarette, and jotted a few more quotes in his notebook before abandoning bystander interviews. Everyone was saying the same thing he'd seen and heard a hundred times before: If he couldn't write the article standing on his head he'd retire. He decided to do some pointed lurking in the vicinity of the video team. He knew how far he could trust his own memory: he wasn't sure how far he could trust that of the team leader. Anyone who could appear in public wearing clothes like that was capable of anything. E. M. Forster blew a wavering stream of smoke into the air and watched it drift between the camera lens and the face of the latest candidate for instant TV stardom.

Rusty Flares emitted a snort. "Cut," came his weary command as he turned to glare at the source of the smoke. He recognised the long, lean form of Forster, and frowned. "Look," he said between his teeth. "*Would* you mind standing back a few miles? We should rather like to get all this under wraps by midnight. If people keep interrupting our best shots . . ."

"Thought you wanted to make the 'Nine o'clock news,' " remarked the seasoned reporter with a lazy grin: But having made his presence known he could afford to retire a short distance, and this he duly did. His retreat was acknowledged with a grudging nod from Rusty Flares as Forster took the cigarette from his mouth and pinched it between forefinger and thumb before sticking it in its usual place behind his ear. He found a handy lamppost against which to incline his grey tweeded length and there inclined, with his hands in his pockets and his hooded eyes watchful.

"From the top again, please." Rusty Flares returned to business. He dodged from one side of the little group to the other, using a fingers-and-thumbs rectangle as a makeshift viewfinder. He nodded. The television hopeful began to speak. E. M. Forster watched and listened.

After a few moments he cleared his throat. The video team froze as their leader cursed. E. M. Forster raised his eyebrows. "Behind you," he said, ignoring the angry looks from all concerned.

"*What?*" snarled Rusty Flares, then saw the direction of Forster's gaze and followed it. "Oh," he said. "Quick!"

The doors of the Allshire and National Bank were being held open by a young policeman to allow a solemn cavalcade, escorted by more uniformed officers, to descend the granite steps. In the van came three paramedics, two carrying a stretcher on which lay a motionless form covered by a red blanket, the third holding up the drip fastened to that motionless form's heavily bandaged left arm.

"Great shot," muttered the video leader as his troops took

aim with their camcorders. "Crowded, though," he added as a second stretcher followed the first. Judging by the hair visible above the blanket, the burden there was female. "Ah," gloated Rusty Flares. "Human interest." He made a note on his clipboard. "Check the hospitals," he murmured and earned a contemptuous look from E. M. Forster.

Oblivious, Rusty Flares continued to watch and his team continued to film as the victims of the shotgun robbery emerged from the insecurity of the bank to the uncertain sanctuary of the outside world. All were pale of face, though some were paler than others. Brisker than most was the gentleman of military aspect who marched beside an elderly woman with a shopping bag in her grasp. A young mother with a bulky dressing on her left temple argued with the ambulance man who wanted to part her from her wailing offspring so that she, too, might rest on a stretcher. Even above the baby's wails the mother's voice was so shrill that enough of her argument was audible to the camcorder team for the leader to gloat again as he made another note about hospitals.

A second, less heavily bandaged head came down the steps. It belonged to a man in horn-rimmed spectacles who walked with a gaze so unfocused that if his lenses had been broken—which they were not—it would have been no surprise. A green-faced youth with red hair ("Hey! Great contrast!") grabbed the bespectacled one when he stumbled.

"What a close-up!" crowed Rusty Flares as the two men staggered together, white face and green, red hair and bloodstained bandage side by side. "Get it!" cried Rusty at the sight of two market traders punching the air and grinning in triumph at their goggling friends below.

"The ambulance!" The first had gunned its engine and was away, its siren blaring, its lights flashing; and now it was the video leader who grinned and punched the air. "Talk about scoops! Eat your heart out, BBC. I'm offering this across the networks! They'll pay thousands!"

E. M. Forster could see the promised stills—his own chance for a scoop—slipping from his grasp. Distasteful or not, there were times when one had to bite the bullet. He cleared his throat as he moved from the lamppost to a position at the rusty one's side. "Remember our quid pro quo?" he enquired, as the second ambulance, pursued by the eager camcorders, sped off after the first.

"What? Oh, the stills." Rusty's tone was vague. "Yes, later . . ." Then he emerged from his daydream of television greatness. "Pro quo what?" came the puzzled echo.

"I could," offered E. M. Forster with only an instant's hesitation, "get you into the hospital. Human interest." He uttered a dry laugh. "Not much I don't know. Not many people, either. I could . . . call in some favours."

"Yeah?" Now Rusty was all attention. "Carry on," he commanded his troops as he led the reporter to one side. "Now, about those stills . . ."

FOR THE MOMENT no more could be done inside the Allshire and National Bank. The bank manager, understandably disoriented by recent events, in his confusion had equated the large stone building with an ocean liner. He would hold to his post on the bridge—that is, in the building—until the last passenger—police officer—was safely off the premises. He sat huddled in a corner by the door to watch the uniformed intruders' every move, from time to time licking ashen lips as he braced himself for the telephone call he would soon have to make to head office.

"Just about done for now, sir." The bank manager jumped as the dejected voice of Superintendent Trewley rumbled at his side. For him to have missed the second coming of that heavy bulldog tread only proved how upset he must be. So much for keeping watch. The telephone call must be preying on his mind.

Stone appeared beside her superior. "You look worse than you did before," she observed kindly. "I think you could do with a stiff drink." Trewley, whose views about drinking on duty were well known, stared at her before he realised the remark had been addressed to the bank manager.

The manager's moan was eloquent. "Well," Stone told him after a quick appraisal, "I don't suppose a small one would do you much harm. Is there by any chance any brandy in your first-aid cupboard?"

The manager babbled weakly of Christmas puddings. Stone nodded. "I won't be long," she promised, and slipped away.

Both men watched her leave in silence. The silence of the bank manager was stunned; Trewley's was approving. "She's a good girl, my sergeant," Trewley said at last, trying to put the poor bloke at his ease. "Medically trained, she is. Bright." He waved a hand to express his admiration for his sergeant's many excellent qualities. "Technical know-how you wouldn't believe." A gusty sigh arose from deep in the bloodhound's throat. "I could swear she's talking a different language sometimes."

"Computers," agreed the bank manager after a pause, forcing a faintly upward twist to the corners of his mouth. "The generation gap." The upward twist became more pronounced, one gap-bridging failure empathising with another. "Most of my staff know more than I ever will about . . ." Then memory returned. "Oh, God!"

"Drink this." Stone had reappeared with a bottle and a glass in her hand. "Yes," she added as the manager opened the eyes he had snapped shut in his anguish. "People really do say it when the need arises. Strong, sweet tea would be better for you, but brandy's quicker."

"The quick—ugh—and the dead." The bank manager, who had taken a swig at his brandy, found it to have achieved a remarkable effect. He swigged again and coughed twice. He felt the colour return to his cheeks. "Thanks, Sergeant."

"It's us who should be thanking you, sir," said Trewley. "For your film," he added as the bank manager blinked at him above the rim of his glasses. "Computer enhancement," he enlarged, in the tones of one leading a forlorn hope. "Our boffins are going to do their damnedest with those security pictures of yours—remember?"

"Oh, God," said the manager again. He'd been doing his best to forget, but people would keep reminding him. He tipped up the glass and drained it. Stone shook her head at his pleading look, and moved the brandy bottle out of sight.

"It's about all we've got to go on so far." Trewley's wistful brown gaze watched the bottle vanish, and he sighed again. "Tracksuits and jeans just like anyone else—and the blighters wore masks, too, didn't they? *And* gloves—not that they really needed 'em, seeing as they made everyone else do the fetching and carrying." He ignored the groan from the man with the empty glass as, rubbing his chin and gazing into the future, he pondered his own misfortune. "Fingerprints are pretty much a waste of time, to be honest. All the ones in here are bound to be legit. Once we find the getaway car we're in with a chance, but—"

Stone, who had been trying to attract the superintendent's attention, now coughed loudly. Trewley broke off with a start. "Yes, well, the security film. Let the forensic blighters play with it, and if they can't tell us what the other blighters looked like, then I'll—I'll—"

"Commandeer the film from the camera crew outside," supplied Stone quickly. "They're bound to have got something we can use. I suggest, sir, that while everyone finishes in here we slip out and . . . and jog people's memories about civic responsibility."

Trewley sighed. She was right: The more film they had to play with, the merrier.

In theory. But theory and practice were far from being the same when science was involved. When things were never as . . . as *certain* as he liked them. If the computer blew a fuse; if some absentminded boffin pressed two buttons in the wrong order, if it came to that, you'd lost the lot. And even if you hadn't, the other side always managed to come up with a boffin who sounded just as impressive as yours. Or as baffling. Juries didn't take kindly to being baffled by jargon, and neither did he. He was an old-fashioned copper. Give him fingerprints over modern technology every time . . .

If only they could find the getaway car.

Four

THE BANK MANAGER looked so bereft as his companions prepared to leave him that Stone allowed her principles to
weaken and poured another small brandy. Trewley stifled an
envious groan, then gave the man an uncharacteristically
encouraging clump on the shoulder before lumbering off
in his sergeant's wake towards the main door. The two
colleagues emerged into the pale spring sunshine and
hesitated on the top step as they looked about them.

"There, sir." Stone pointed to the little group of camcord-
ing experts bustling among the market stalls. One of the
group was issuing crisp instructions through megaphoned
hands. "He'll be the one we want."

"Ugh." Trewley did not approve of men who wore fancy
suits, with or without polka-dot cravats. Polka-dots were for
handkerchiefs and, at a pinch, the occasional necktie. "Want
him? I wouldn't have him as a gift."

"We aren't asking him to *give* them to us," Stone said,
deliberately mishearing as the pair made their way down the
steps. "A friendly loan, that's all. For copying purposes. It
shouldn't take too long once we've reached the lab."

"Especially if we call ahead for the blighters to expect
them," Trewley said, brightening somewhat. As he brightened, Stone in her turn grew dejected. Visions of the car in
dry dock yet again as the superintendent contrived for the
umpteenth time to put her radio out of action floated across
her inward eye. How a man otherwise so good at his job

could so dismally fail to have the knack for pushing a
simple switch to the left had, to her, long been a source of
glum bewilderment.

But she said nothing as they reached the bottom step and
threaded their stoic passage between the stalls to where an
absorbed Rusty Flares, watched from a distance by the silent
E. M. Forster, was making more notes on his clipboard. The
journalist raised a lazy hand in greeting. Trewley nodded an
acknowledgement; Stone offered a quick smile of courtesy,
then waited for her chief to speak.

"Excuse me, sir." The bulldog was trying not to sound
fierce. "Would these cameras be your responsibility?"

With the exasperated click of his tongue Rusty Flares
looked up from the clipboard. "Oh, really! We'll never get
this under wraps if we keep being interrupted." He shot a
darkling look in the direction of the watching Forster. "My
cameras? What if they are?"

"We're police officers, sir . . ." Trewley fumbled in his
jacket pocket for his identification.

"Police?" At once Rusty was all smiling cooperation.
"We—I—wrote for permission to film," he said, showing
flawless teeth above the pink polka-dots. "You're not going
to change your minds now, are you?"

"Not," said Trewley with an ominous chuckle to show he
didn't mean it, "so long as you let us borrow what you've
got of the business at the bank."

"What?"

"Come now, sir, you must have got something. You aren't
telling me you've been here all morning and missed the
biggest piece of news we've had in Allingham for months."
The superintendent strove to remember the jargon. "A
scoop, and you right on the spot—there isn't a cameraman
in England would pass up a chance like that."

"The Nine O'Clock News," observed E. M. Forster in a
loud voice to nobody in particular. Trewley nodded another
acknowledgement as Stone smothered a grin.

Rusty Flares winced. "Look, um, Inspector." He squinted
at the identity card still being held under his nose. "I'm
sorry. Superintendent." He favoured Stone—of the same

generation as himself and female, to boot—with a whimsical smile. He did not even attempt to check her identification. "Look," he said again, man to man. Stone frowned.

He ignored her. "The thing is, Superintendent," he said in honeyed accents, "in the normal way I'd be only too happy to cooperate with the police right away, but you said yourself we've got a scoop here. If you could only wait until tomorrow—"

"We can't," Trewley told him.

"But we'll lose our advantage if you take it now!" The clipboard was brandished in an agitated manner. "Tomorrow, first thing," said Rusty Flares. "I promise."

"Withholding evidence," said Stone thoughtfully as her superior's bulldog glare fastened on the polka-dot cravat, and he scowled.

The wearer of the cravat took two hurried steps back. "I'm not!" he protested, sounding uncertain.

"No, you're not," agreed Trewley, sounding more than sure of himself. "Because we're going to help you. To help us. With our enquiries," he added, taking his own turn at teeth-baring in a far from smiling manner. "My sergeant here will drive the whole bunch of you, cameras and all, to our lab the minute we've done talking, Mr. . . . ?"

"Pearce," said he of the needlecord, polka-dots, and poor colour sense, in tones of deep resignation. "Piers Pearce— Pearce Productions, you know." As Trewley had done, he patted his pockets in an automatic gesture before coming just in time to his senses.

"No, sir, I don't," Trewley said. "Pearce Productions? Film, no doubt. Not exactly in my line. But all we want just now is for you to *produce* whatever's in those cameras of yours for us to look at before anyone else does. The boffins will sort out everything for you—develop your film, or whatever needs doing, at top speed." Piers Pearce opened his mouth, then shut it again. "Run off a copy or two," Trewley went on, aware that he was approaching dangerous ground. "For computer enhancement. But that needn't worry you," he added hurriedly. "Once we've had 'em copied you can have 'em back for every news channel in the country, with my blessing. Sell 'em abroad, if you want. But *we* want to look at them first. So the sooner you accept Sergeant Stone's kind offer of a lift, the sooner you can start telephoning the telly people to put in their bids, or whatever they do. All right?"

Piers Pearce drew in his breath. "All right," he said. "I suppose there's not much more we can reasonably do around here now things are calming down. Give us two minutes, Sergeant, and we're with you."

"More time lost," said Trewley as Stone did her own spot of pocket-patting for the car keys. "Better catch up on the way, Sergeant." He scowled again at the polka-dot cravat and the elegantly casual lines of the needlecord suit. "Blues and twos, I think."

"Sir," said Stone, straight-faced and noncommittal. She thought it unfair of the superintendent to ask her to submit the entire camcorder team to the battery of flashing beacons and yodelling sirens when it was only their leader who had actively annoyed him.

And her. She looked again at Piers Pearce, remembering how he had looked—or rather hadn't—at her. Then she looked beyond him to the others of his team who were rallying meekly to their master's call. Guilt by association. A faint smile curved her lips. Unfair? Perhaps not. Blues and twos . . .

Trewley watched the car speed off in a flurry of light and double-barrelled screaming. An evil grin creased the bull-dog face. Serve the blighter right. If he wanted his blasted scoop, let him suffer for it like everyone else . . .

The grin faded. Blighter or not, Pearce wouldn't suffer half as much as those poor devils in hospital on the danger list. The superintendent muttered something very rude about thugs in general and the Allingham bank robbers in particular as he strode back up the steps. If only they could find the getaway car . . .

THE BOFFINS HAD spoken learnedly and at length of clean-image technology and digital analysis, but when pressed had promised the photos—both bank and camcorder—by the end of the day. It seemed those hours would never pass.

Trewley checked statements and compared notes and came up with wild theories he dared Stone to shoot down. Wise beyond her years, she did not dare. He ground his teeth every time the telephone rang on his desk and it wasn't a boffin calling to say a messenger could be sent to collect the stills, it was somebody else whose call (according to the superintendent) should have been cut off long before it reached him, and if he could only spare the time to get his hands on that fool on the switchboard . . .

Stone murmured an excuse and left the room for a tactful word with the switchboard operator. The ensuing silence magnified the tick of the clock on the office wall into a relentless rhythmic thunder of accusation.

"Five to five," growled Trewley, glaring at the wall as if the clock itself were to blame for the silence. "Those lazy blighters will be knocking off any minute now—and where the hell does that leave us?"

The clock had never kept proper time. Stone couldn't help herself; she checked her wristwatch. Trewley saw her checking and shot her a furious look. She decided she might as well be hanged for a sheep as for a lamb. "They won't have finished work just yet, sir, but in any case they'll be doing overtime on this assignment if it isn't quite ready. They promised me—"

"Promises?" snarled Trewley. "Blasted piecrust—made to be broken!"

Stone hid a smile: He was always more irascible as time (and his latest diet) went on. "They wouldn't dare break this particular promise," she assured him gravely. "I, um, took the liberty of telling them you would have their guts for garters if they let us down."

"Charming language, Detective Sergeant Stone."

"Imitation is the sincerest form of flattery, sir."

"Umph." The bulldog slumped in his chair, brooding. He looked up and saw the twinkle in her eye. "Well," he began.

The telephone rang. Trewley leaped for his receiver; Stone leaped for hers. The voice at the other end of the line greeted them cheerfully before telling them what they had waited several hours to hear. "Come and get it," they were told. "Unless you'd prefer to hang on half an hour or so and save yourself the bother, that is. One of our crowd lives in your neck of the woods. He could drop the package off on his way home—"

"We'll fetch it ourselves!" Trewley banged down the receiver and glanced across at Stone. "Not one word from you, my girl," he warned as the twinkle brightened to a mischievous gleam. "After the afternoon I've had I'm only too glad to get out of this madhouse for a while."

"So I gather." Stone was shrugging on the jacket she had draped over the back of her chair. In its pocket the car keys jangled gaily. "If you're even prepared to take a chance on my driving . . ."

"If you blue-and-two it the way you did before," he told her as they hurried together from the office, "I'll have you busted to traffic before you can blink."

"But—sir, I thought we were in a hurry." Stone had darted ahead to hold open the heavy swing door leading to the car park. "If we want to make tonight's television and tomorrow's papers with the enhanced pictures, I mean."

Trewley said nothing until they were buckled into their seat belts and the car was nosing its way out of the station yard into the road. "We won't," he said heavily.

It took her only an instant to divine his meaning. "We can try," she said bracingly.

"No point," he told her. "Be realistic, girl. What's a bank robbery nowadays when the world's full of terrorists and serial killers and—and fornicating politicians to make the headlines?"

"People were killed here, too, sir," she reminded him gravely. "That have-a-go market trader in the bank, and the man they knocked over in the street, and other people are on the danger list. Doesn't that count for something?"

"It should," he replied, "but it won't. The best hope we've got, damn him, is Piers Pearce and his action replay scoop. Granted he wasn't bothered about the blighters when they went *into* the bank because they weren't making a blasted exhibition of themselves—but he noticed them coming out, all right. And got enough of 'em on film, even if they *were* wearing masks, to make it worth a telly editor's while to show some of it on the news." He eased himself into a more comfortable position as the car swung around a corner. "And maybe someone'll recognise the way one of 'em runs or something. I hate to say it, Stone, but we could live to be grateful to that polka-dotted perisher yet . . ."

OVER THE YEARS, Desk Sergeant Pleate had seen it all; and heard it, too. If the loonies didn't pop in personally to make their idiotic complaints, it was only because they were on the telephone bending his ear about Martians on the golfcourse or wife-swapping in the house next door or conspirators signalling to one another by pegging up their washing in a different daily order on the line.

Over the years Pleate had come to know (though not to love) his loonies. The Major, for instance, with his fixation about the stuffed animals on the windowsill of the nursery in the house three doors from his own, was easily deflected. Big Game Hunting is a sensitive issue in these conservationist days, but if Pleate was willing to concede that (a) the tiger had indeed been despatched by a masterly shot from the Major and (b) those who insisted there were no tigers in Africa had missed the point, because it had been the Major who exterminated them, then the old Empire-builder would march happily on his way, twirling his moustache and saying that his solicitor (known by Pleate to have retired a decade ago) would be writing to the neighbour in question to demand the return of his stolen property.

Eccentric they might be, but Pleate had never regarded the Clench sisters as likely loonies. The Clench sisters were identical twins. Even Pleate could never tell which was which from voice or appearance alone. It was only when they introduced themselves that anyone found out, for the elder was always the correct "Miss Clench" while her cadet was always the equally correct "Miss Prudence." Miss Prudence never made any reference more specific than "my dear sister," but rumour—fuelled by a rarity of ancients who had shared the Clench girls' Edwardian schooldays—held that Miss Clench had been christened Charity.

Charitable (and prudent) the Clench sisters undoubtedly were. They were also, in the nature of things, advanced in years, but so far age did not seem to have wearied them. Their eyes were bright; their hearing was keen. Their noses had raised the alarm in the matter of the crossroads gas leak long before officialdom confirmed its presence with the help of the latest technology. The Clench sisters read *The Times* and *The Daily Telegraph* each day, and daily took it in turns to do the crossword puzzles, which they courageously completed in fountain pen rather than pusillanimous pencil. They had, in short, all their marbles: But Pleate knew that marbles could be treacherous, and easily lost . . .

"A complaint, Miss Clench?" Pleate adjusted the telephone on his shoulder, reached out to pull the Occurrence Book—open at a fresh page for a new day—across the counter, and picked up a ballpoint pen. "Can you tell me what the trouble seems to be?"

"Men," said Miss Clench crisply. Pleate's heart sank. "Taking their clothes off," said Miss Clench, "in the road outside my house—a sufficiently abnormal activity, even in these free-living times, to merit police interest, I would have thought."

"Er," said Sergeant Pleate, abandoning the Occurrence Book for the jotting pad beside it. *Unmarried ladies*, he thought. *Men*, he wrote. "Yes, I grant you, it does sound . . . odd," he said. "How about some details, now?"

Miss Clench sighed. "I fear I am unable to give as many as I should wish," she said apologetically. "It was my dear sister who noticed these men, not I."

"Ah," said Sergeant Pleate. "Your sister."

"She is resting at present," Miss Clench informed him. "The aftermath of a severe migraine that started yesterday afternoon. We are both subject to these attacks, although fortunately never at the same time . . ."

"Yes," said Sergeant Pleate. *Sick fancies*, he thought.

"The only cure we have found that is at all efficacious, beyond the pills prescribed by our general practitioner, is for the victim to lie down as soon as possible in a darkened room. My sister became aware just before luncheon that an attack was impending. She went straight upstairs, naturally, and before drawing her bedroom curtains looked out of the window to see if I might be on my way home." As with their crossword puzzles, the Clench twins were known to keep house on a turn-and-turn-about basis. After sharing the lighter duties each morning (they had a weekly woman for the rough) one sister would prepare and cook the midday meal while the other made her stately way to the local corner shop to buy groceries and the day's papers, to be enjoyed at the twins' leisure over past-prandial coffee and a small glass of medicinal port for each.

"And were you on your way home?" asked Pleate politely.

"For my poor sister's sake I regret that I was not," said Miss Clench. "But it was as she looked for me before closing the curtains that she saw the men in the road."

"Taking their clothes off." Pleate's flat echo of Miss Clench's earlier words was accompanied by a faint sigh.

"Exactly so," said Miss Clench, her voice sharpening as she recognised the sigh for what it was. "Neither my sister nor I, Sergeant, is given to hysterical imaginings, and—"

"Of course, Miss Clench. I'm sorry." Pleate did his best to sound as if he meant it. The Clench family had been prominent in Allshire affairs for the past century or more. They might be the last of their line, but the elderly twins still had several influential ears willing to hear them. He coughed as Miss Clench returned a brief acknowledgement of his apology. "I'm sorry," he said in a different tone, "but I don't understand why all this wasn't reported yesterday, if you—she—found it so disturbing. Whatever," he found himself adding, "it was."

Miss Clench replied in icy accents: " 'It,' Sergeant, was four men removing their outer garments in what can only be described as a surreptitious manner behind the tree outside the house next door to ours. You may recall"—the ice did not melt: Miss Clench seemed to suggest that she doubted him capable of recollection—"how the grass verge of our road on both sides is planted with some venerable sycamores." It was Miss Clench's turn to cough. "Trees more venerable even than my sister and myself, Sergeant."

"I'm sorry, Miss Clench, but I—"

"No doubt," said Miss Clench, raising her voice above his faint protestation, "these men selected that tree above the rest because it has the largest trunk. They might have supposed themselves to run little risk of being observed in their bizarre activities—this is a quiet side road, Sergeant, with hardly any through traffic. As you will recall."

"Er—yes, Miss Clench," said Desk Sergeant Pleate, terror of the Allingham police force.

"Quite so." The temperature rose slightly now that the sergeant had been brought to heel. "As to why you were not informed of this occurrence earlier, it is that by the time I returned from my excursion, my poor sister, under the influence of her medication, had fallen soundly asleep. Knitting up the ravell'd sleave of care, Sergeant. The balm of hurt minds."

Barmy, thought Sergeant Pleate, but he did not speak one syllable aloud.

"Despite her night's rest she was still somewhat muzzy this morning," Miss Clench continued to inform the now dubious silence on the other end of the line. "Naturally, once she had regained full control of her faculties, she told me what she had seen yesterday. She saw," Miss Clench went on as the silence continued, "four men, who had apparently driven up in a dark blue car, removing their—"

"In a *what*? What did you say?" cried Pleate.

"To have begun to lose your hearing at so comparatively young an age must cause you considerable distress, Sergeant. You have my sympathy." Was that a note of amusement in the voice of the elder Miss Clench? "My sister," she enunciated clearly, "observed four men in the act of removing their loose-fitting over-jackets—from her description I would say these were what are known as tracksuit tops—to reveal more, ah, formally casual clothing underneath. Check shirts and, ah, sweatshirts, I believe the correct term to be."

"Go on," prompted Sergeant Pleate as she hesitated, no doubt searching a vocabulary widened by decades of crossword puzzling for a term yet more correct.

"Although her eyesight was by this time far from steady, she saw the men place these . . . baggy tops inside the boots of three cars parked in the sycamore shade—perhaps with some idea of keeping them cool should the sun chance to shine. Which, as you will recall, yesterday it seldom did."

"No," agreed Sergeant Pleate. "I mean, yes. I mean—so what did she see next?"

"Nothing," said Miss Clench. A groan escaped the sergeant's anguished lips. "Except flashing lights," added Miss Clench in the interest of accuracy. "She had closed the curtains by this time and was lying down." The explanation was spoken in tones of utter reasonableness. "She could, however, despite the pain in her head, make out the sound of doors slamming and the engines, ah, revving as the cars drove away. All three of them," she concluded, as Pleate emitted another groan and ground his teeth.

"How," he brought out, "can she be sure they all drove away together? If she was feeling so poorly by then."

"Because she recalls remarking how strange it was to have four cars so close together in our quiet street," said Miss Clench. "When she first noticed the men, that is. By the time I arrived home I saw only one. It must be the car in which the men drove here for the exchange, if I have the term correctly. When they return, I intend to speak to them about the inconsiderate manner in which they have left it blocking our neighbour's drive. It is fortunate that she is housebound, otherwise—"

"What did you say?" cried Pleate again; then, before she could goad him further about his hearing, demanded: "Do you mean to tell me that car is still outside your house?"

"Outside our neighbour's house," amended the accurate Miss Clench. "Yes."

"Stay there!" cried Pleate. "Don't move! There'll be somebody at your place in five minutes!"

Unless he was very much mistaken, the getaway car was found.

Five

UNLIKE MOST OF their neighbours—unlike, indeed, most of the populace of Britain—the Misses Clench owned no television set. They knew from observation in the streets of Allingham that police cars sometimes travelled with sirens blaring and blue lights flashing. They might, from their wide choice of reading matter, guess that the drivers of these cars would communicate by radio in the same way that the bobby on the beat often had cause to do. The Misses Clench were elderly, but they were far from out of touch.

And yet, for all their perspicacity, they did not for a moment suspect that the arrival of two panda cars and an unmarked vehicle from the forensic science laboratory would arouse even half the interest that it did among local residents so much more accustomed than themselves to having seen it all before in the privacy of their homes, and now only too eager to observe it in close-up reality within a quarter of a mile of those same homes.

"It's just like *Z Cars*—just like *Z Cars*!" enthused someone whose favourite viewing period had been some time in the 1960s. The woman police officer who had been first to arrive in response to Sergeant Pleate's alert tried to send a preliminary report via her car radio, but was forced to raise her voice that she might hear herself think. The voice on the other end of the radio advised her primly that there was no need to shout.

"That's all you know," came the sour retort of the WPC, who was then rebuked for indiscipline on the airwaves.

"Car 54, where are you?" chuckled someone else whose memory went even further into the televisual mists.

"If you could just move back a little, please . . ." The man who had chuckled found himself being edged out of the way by a member of the forensic team, a young woman armed with a camera who was bent on taking photographs of the dark blue car from every possible direction. Some of her uniformed colleagues were busy securing the area with plastic cones and lengths of nylon ribbon; others were preparing to knock on people's doors and ask what—if anything—they had seen of the abandoned vehicle's movements, and those of its occupants, during the previous day.

They were not especially sanguine in this endeavour. Piers Pearce's film of the bank robbery had made prime-time national television news on both main channels the night before. Piers was a happy man that morning (as was his bank manager, who after hearing from his client had decided to reconsider the stiff letter he had been going to write about Mr. Pearce's overdraft). But, though the telephones had started ringing at Allingham police station the moment the scene had changed from the flight of the gang from the scene of the crime to the stumbling down the granite steps of the pale-faced hostages with their police and paramedic escorts, not a soul from the Clenches' part of town had rung in to add anything to the welter of speculation that had gripped everyone else for miles around.

The Misses Clench were unique in far more than their advanced age and domestic eccentricity. Apart from their housebound neighbour, theirs was the only establishment in the road where the adult inhabitants did not go out to work. Yesterday morning, when the three cars seen by Prudence must have been parked before the robbery, the rest of the potential witnesses had been at work; as, indeed, they were today. The neighbours who hovered nearby making asinine remarks about *Softly, Softly* and *The Bill* had been drawn as moths to a flame from surrounding streets by the blue flashing lights of the police cars; yet, not a curtain in the road where the Clench sisters lived had so much as twitched during the commotion. Nobody, the investigative forces feared, would, once caught at home in the evening, have anything useful to tell them . . .

"TYPICAL," SNARLED SUPERINTENDENT Trewley as he scanned the first reports and hurled them to one side. On Stone's desk the paperwork rustled and lifted in the angry breeze. "Talk about ignorance is bliss, my girl." He stabbed the air with his forefinger. "That lot must be the happiest blasted bunch in town!"

"Unlike us," observed Stone, sotto voce.

"I heard that." The superintendent slammed a cardboard folder shut and threw it on his growing reject pile. The pile teetered, but stayed firm. "Just tell me what you think we've got to be happy *about*, for pity's sake. Never mind the robbery itself, we've had damned bad luck right through the—the aftermath." The bloodhound eyes were raised lugubriously to the ceiling as he prepared to catalogue his woes. "It wasn't mentioned on national radio, and the Clench girls never listen to the local station. They don't have television, so they didn't see it last night."

"Lots of people did, sir."

The interruption was ignored. "Twelve hours we've lost—*twelve hours*—because those two don't have their papers delivered. They like the fresh air and the company and they don't read the things until after lunch . . ."

"But Forensics say they'll be as quick as they can—and it's not as if the car was vandalised overnight, remember." Stone tried to sound cheerful. "Any traces that were left there yesterday will still be there today, sir. And Prue couldn't tell us much more than her sister told Sergeant Pleate this morning, could she? Migraines," said the former medical student, "can be ghastly. I'm only thankful our flashing blues didn't give the poor woman another attack when she's barely over the last."

"Umph." Trewley tipped back his chair on two legs so that it was easier to stare at the ceiling. "Anything about what the pair of 'em said make you wonder, Stone?"

"They said a great deal," she returned warily. "But if you're thinking of deluded old maids, my semiprofessional view is that they aren't."

"That's not what I meant." The chair came down with a thump. The topmost file slithered from its place and started a small avalanche of paperwork. Trewley, theorising, for once did not curse it. "They kept on about what a quiet, respectable street it's always been."

Stone was more puzzled now than wary. "Well—yes, it has. And apart from the car, it still is. Everyone says so, not just the Clench twins. Our beat blokes, the neighbours—everyone."

"A car or two they don't recognise must be legitimate visitors," said Trewley. "That's what they'd think. Relatives, the doctor—no, they'd recognise the doc's car—but a quiet, well-managed, private sort of street. Right?"

"Yes, sir. It's not on a direct route, of course . . ." Stone stared at her superior, whose corrugated face was creased still more in a sudden massive grin. "Oh," said Stone. "Yes, of course. Um—are you thinking what I'm thinking, sir?"

"Got to be local," said Trewley, and she nodded. "Your Young What's-His-Name," he went on. Stone winced. There had been a considerable explosion yesterday when her superior learned of her partner's close encounter with the dark blue car. Holding her breath, she was relieved to see that the grin had not faded. It might almost have been thought that the bulldog was chuckling. "Biggest banana fritter in the world, didn't he say? Snarled up the traffic lights for Lord knows how long."

"*I* know," muttered Stone, whose sleep the previous night had been much disturbed.

"An eyewitness to the getaway," said Trewley, "that's what he is. A trained observer, heaven help us, but what did he see?" He gave her no time to answer. "Car going at full speed, overtakes a line of traffic, spots the hold-up almost too late, realises it can't get past, turns round and heads off down another road out of town . . ."

"And finds its way straight to where the other cars were waiting," supplied Stone. "From what Miss Prudence has said, they really can't have wasted any time getting lost, even though all those little side streets are terribly confusing to a stranger. So, local . . ."

"Local," Trewley agreed. He was pleased that she had come unprompted to the same conclusion, though he would have expected no less. "And not born-here-and-moved-away local," he added. "That one-way system's been changed in the last twelve months, remember."

Stone remembered only too well. The period in question had been another of her nightmare experiences. She sighed.

Trewley, rubbing his chin, grinned at her again. "Yes. Local, then. Even the best driver in the business doesn't— can't—plan half a dozen escape routes in case one of 'em's blocked. Anyone with brains enough for that's got too much sense to go in for crime in the first place—"

"We hope," said Stone before he could say it himself.

"Er—yes." Trewley blinked at her. His years in the force had left him with few illusions about the criminal mentality. He had always regarded Stone as far too optimistic about human nature, and it surprised him now that she seemed for once to be endorsing his own more cynical point of view. "Yes," he agreed, rallying. "Some of 'em'll go to the bad no matter what. Fact of life. Still—a Mr. Big in Allingham? I suppose it's always possible, but . . ."

"No matter how big he was," said Stone, "and how skilled a team he could afford to put together, local or not, he'd never have risked a driver who wasn't local. Imagine a—a foreigner letting one of his passengers shout last-minute instructions at him when he's driving hell-for-leather down an unknown road. It's simply not on, sir."

"You're right. It isn't. So, whatever leads we get for the rest of the blighters, we know the driver must be one of ours." The superintendent pushed back his chair and stood up. "Time for a break, my girl. Tea and buns and a breath of fresh air—and then we get back to the mugshots and the statements. And we start putting the word round the local snouts that we're interested in anything they know . . ." He frowned. "As if they need telling. If they didn't see it on Pearce's perishing video, they'll have been on the phone

straight after the event to let their mates know that someone's making easy money in my manor, and he's not too
fussy about how many people get hurt in the making . . ."

THE STAFF OF the *Allingham Argus*, which went to press on
Thursday mornings, had worked overtime through Wednesday
night to adapt the front page to include E. M. Forster's as yet
brief account of the Bank Robbery Sensation. Next Friday's
paper, readers were promised, would include in-depth interviews with eyewitnesses, plus a wider selection of the still
photographs supplied by the video team providentially on the
spot at the time of the outrage. A smudged footnote added just
as the papers were about to be bundled up for distribution gave
an update of the condition of such victims as had been
admitted to hospital.

   Those dead, on the danger list, or with a Human Interest
angle to their stories had rather more journalistic glamour
than those who had neither risked their lives to protect the
innocent, nor been struck down by ironic Fate in the robbery
aftermath as had the man who, brooding on redundancy and
caught by the wing of the car, was thrown backwards to
smash his skull on the market cobbles.

   One of those less glamorous victims was Paul Ross, the
bewildered man in horn-rimmed spectacles who had staggered down the steps of the raided bank with the red-haired
youth beside him. Youth is more resilient than middle age.
Once in hospital the redhead had made a speedy recovery,
taking advantage of his admission to Casualty to chat up
(with some success) two of the student nurses assigned to
the group of shocked yet vertical people whose physical
injuries could be regarded as less urgent than those of
others, horizontal on stretchers, rushed straight to the
operating theatre.

   The unfortunate Ross, knocked out by the Regular
Savings advertisement board when the overhead Interest
Rates placard crashed into it, had regained just enough
strength of mind to be able to walk more or less unaided
from the bank, but in Casualty had collapsed again to slump,

silent and stunned, as the emergency dressing on his head was removed for X-ray purposes.

A doctor asked how many fingers she was holding up. Her patient could only stare at her and sigh.

The doctor shone a torch in his eyes. He blinked, but slowly. The doctor clicked her tongue, then made rather more reassuring noises as she carried out further tests. These, however, only served to confirm her preliminary diagnosis of mild concussion. With a scribble of her signature, the admission of Paul Ross to Men's Surgical for observation was authorised.

Ross had spent the rest of Wednesday in fitful slumber. He spent most of Thursday undergoing another round of tests before discharging himself (against doctor's orders) in the evening because he was apprehensive about taking too much time off work. The shadow of redundancy spread far and wide across Allshire. The firm for which he worked operated a "Last In, First Out" policy theoretically fair, but realistically hard on the nervous system of one who had been there for less than three years.

On Friday morning, his hair brushed carefully over his thinning scalp to hide the square of sticking plaster that was the most visible souvenir of his recent hospital experience, Paul Ross drove to work. He avoided main roads and kept—for almost the first time in his life—within the speed limit for the entire journey. It wasn't so much he believed for a minute that the doctor had been right—of course it wasn't—but there was no sense in taking risks.

"Give us yer autograph, and I might just let you in," came the greeting from the security man on the gate. The puzzled Ross shook his head—which made him wince—and could find nothing to say in reply. "Hoity-toity!" scoffed the security man, cranking up the barrier just high enough for the car to edge its way underneath. He let it down again with no more than six inches' clearance at the back. Ross, seeing without seeing in the rearview mirror, winced again and drove on to find a space.

Ross's normal practice was to reverse in so that anyone blocking him could be more easily out-manoeuvred. On this occasion, for some reason he would not admit to himself, he decided to park nose-first. More easily. Safely.

There came a crunch, a jolt, and an unpleasing jangling sound from the passenger side. Paul Ross watched his nearside wing mirror splinter to the ground in the close embrace of the driver's mirror from the car next to his.

"Oh, damn." It was all he could find the strength to say. "Oh, damn . . ."

He climbed out of the car and glanced in the direction of the gate. The security man was watching him, bright-eyed and curious. No point in moving to another spot, then. When challenged by the owner of the neighbouring vehicle, he would have to own up.

He remembered the crunch and the jolt. He went to the front of his car. He saw the crumpled bumper and the broken glass, and cursed again.

"Oh, damn . . ." He blinked away the fog from inside his spectacles and took a deep breath. Back to work. This lot had to be paid for. He could do without having to fill in a wodge of insurance forms and having to answer a load of questions, not to mention losing his no-claims bonus . . .

"Paul— Hey, Paul!" Running feet thumped on asphalt, making his eyeballs quiver as sparks danced before them. That doctor *hadn't* been right—*she hadn't*—but . . .

"Paul, great to see you back! How's it going? Hey," said the speaker as he drew closer, "you don't look so good, if you don't mind me saying so."

"Dean." The nod with which Mr. Ross hailed the younger man made the sparks dance again. "I feel fine, thanks." He took another deep breath, straightened bowed shoulders, and began striding towards the entrance of the building that suddenly seemed so very far away.

He realised he was walking, no longer striding. *But that doctor was wrong!* His legs hesitated for a moment . . .

Dean adjusted his own, more youthful step. "You really should've left coming in until Monday," he said. "We'd have understood, but—hey." Dean was chortling now. "How's it feel to be a star?"

"What?" Ross found his legs hesitating again. Without a

word, his escort grabbed him by the arm and helped him up three low steps and through the main office door.

"Oooh, Paul!" The girl on reception greeted his appearance with the widest smile she'd ever given him. "Ooh, I say, can I touch you?"

"What?" Ross shook off Dean's alien touch from his elbow. "What are you talking about?"

"You're famous," said the receptionist as Dean guffawed beside him. "Trust you to be where the action is! I always said you had . . . hidden depths." Mascara speckled the snowy curves of her bosom as she batted her eyelashes at him in a self-mocking show of admiration.

"What?" said Ross for the third time. The room seemed to be moving in a peculiar way. Why was Dean grabbing him by the arm? Why was that stupid girl gaping at him? What was she burbling about chairs?

"Here, mate, sit down." Dean dragged him over to the low leather settle against the wall. "I *said* you didn't ought to've come in today . . ."

"Is that our local hero?" Other voices joined the whirling babble. "Paul, hello! You look a bit rough . . ."

". . . too much for him, I told him so . . ."

". . . lucky to be in one piece, considering . . ."

". . . sick note until Monday, easy . . ."

". . . be in Hollywood by then . . ."

Everyone roared with laughter. The sound brought the subject of the discussion out of his daze. "What—what the hell is everyone talking about?" he cried. "There's no need to fuss—I'm fine!"

"You don't look it," observed someone as his hand rose instinctively to his spectacles and snatched them off. That baffled outburst had made the sparks do their wildest dance yet. Paul Ross buried his face in his hands and groaned.

"He's not well," said the receptionist. "I'll phone for the nurse. It's an emergency!"

"He needs air," said someone else, snatching up one of those mysterious glossy magazines that are only ever found in waiting areas. He flapped it up and down near Paul's face. The reluctant invalid flinched in the sudden breeze, and his hair slipped away from the hitherto hidden square of sticking plaster.

"Wow," somebody said as there was a general intake of breath. "Honourable wounds, eh?"

"It doesn't look half as bad as it did on the telly," argued someone jealous of the anxious looks being cast in Paul's direction by the receptionist, who was still busy on the telephone. "Making too much fuss, that's what it was. The great bandage, and now just—"

"Telly?" cried Paul Ross, opening his eyes and jerking bolt upright. His face was a sickly green, his mouth the yellowish white of badly curdled cream. He licked his lips. "Wh-what do you mean?"

"We all saw you," came the chorus. "Knew you at once—couldn't mistake—famous for fifteen minutes—tell us all about it, mate—nothing like a spot of excitement, eh?"

Too much excitement, Paul Ross might have replied; but he did not—could not—answer. Jerking himself out of his state of shock must have been the final straw. With a low, whimpering groan he let the horn-rimmed spectacles slip from his fingers and slid, grey-faced and fainting, to the floor.

"There," said Dan with grim satisfaction. "Didn't I try telling him? I *knew* he shouldn't have come back to work till after the weekend!"

Six

FRIDAY WAS TRADITIONALLY Funnies' Day at the police station, for it was on Friday mornings that the *Allingham Argus* came out. Allshire would have to be on its collective deathbed for its citizens to leave reading the *Argus* for later. Even when the pressure of their workload was at its most extreme, Trewley and Stone seldom failed to take time at elevenses (if not sooner) to pursue this comprehensive reportage of local doings great and small. A nod could be as good as a wink, a judicious phrase as good as a ten-minute telephone call to warn of trouble. In common with the rest of the county, the guardians of its peace liked to know as far in advance as possible what the opposition might be plotting before too much damage could be done.

The damage to the Allshire and National Bank had been done already.

"Now I'd call that pretty smart reporting," said Stone, who had temporarily abandoned her own in favour of Trewley's visitors' chair. "For a front page scoop in the *Argus*." She put down her share of the paper and picked up a chocolate biscuit from the plate that lay between piles of as yet unfiled documentation on Trewley's blotter, where they could both comfortably reach it. By tacit consent the superintendent's wife and his sergeant had seen fit to dispense with all dietary constraints for the duration.

Trewley grunted as he swapped his half of the paper for Stone's and began re-reading. "Forster knows his stuff." He scowled at the Stop Press column with its update on those in hospital. "And so do the blighters who did the blasted job, damn them."

"But only in the sense that the car was left relatively clean," Stone ventured to remind him. "Plus the local knowledge, of course. But if they'd really known what they were doing they would have had the sense to know we'd be after them twice as fast when it was a question of murder and grievous bodily harm, not just a—an ordinary hold-up."

"None of 'em's got any sense. They're all fools—and they aren't the only ones."

Stone sighed. She would not quickly be allowed to forget the views of her superior on that unfortunate sighting of the getaway car at the gas board roadworks. She tried to look on the bright side. "At least Forster hasn't tried to make fools of—of us, sir. He's been fair. None of those 'Are the police asleep on the job?' headlines a real Grub Streeter could never have resisted."

The bulldog flashed her a look. "Meaning you think I've been a bit unfair in certain respects?"

"It's hardly my place to comment, sir."

"Meekness doesn't suit you, Stone." Trewley helped himself to another biscuit. "D'you reckon it's worth ringing the hospital again?"

"They said," said Stone, "they would tell us the minute anyone was well enough to make a statement. As they haven't—well, they can't be, can they? Sir."

Trewley swallowed the last mouthful. "And that's your expert medical opinion." He began to brush crumbs off the newspaper into his wastepaper bin.

"For what it's worth when I haven't set eyes on any of the patients, yes." Stone pulled the packet of biscuits across the blotter, and started pleating the hollow cellophane into folds that would lie flat. "I should think," she offered after a pause broken only by crisp crinkling sounds, "the best person to ask, if you can't ask the nursing staff, could be E. M. Forster. He's always bragging about his sources and how he knows what's going on almost before it happens—and he does."

"Umph. How that man gets his information sometimes I'll never know." Trewley sighed as Stone cut a neat strip of sticky tape to make an air-proof seal. "We could do with some of his—his sources ourselves right now. Ours have been about as much blasted use as binoculars would have been to Nelson."

"Before or after the battle of Calvi, sir?"

Another look flashed her way from beneath the bulldog brow. "If I had a telescope, my girl, I'd brain you with it for cheek and risk the consequences." Trewley sighed again as his sergeant grinned, rose nimbly from his visitors' chair, and took the biscuits and herself away. "Maybe this rag"—here the superintendent brandished the innocent *Argus* with an irritable hand—"will jog a few memories." He snorted. "Persuade a few honest citizens to do their bit for the community."

"Maybe the bank will think about a reward," suggested Stone as she began to rummage among the cardboard folders on her desk. "Or maybe Forensic will come up with more evidence. It's early days yet, sir. Think positive."

Trewley was feeling decidedly negative about the progress—or lack of it—of the case so far, and was about to say so when the adjective she had used set him off on a new train of thought.

Back, rather, to one he had tried more than once before, and had more than once abandoned. "*Early* days?" he snapped. "Two days—forty-eight hours—they've had, but we mustn't give up on the computer enhancements, must we? Must give the boffins a chance to earn their keep . . ." He did his own spot of folder rummaging. "Well, something might just come of them after all this time." He didn't need to add "But I doubt it." His tone made this very plain. Stone did not bother to answer him.

"Umph." He removed the spectacles he had worn to study the *Argus*, and let his eyes drift in and out of focus in a manner to alarm anyone who didn't know what he was doing as he rocked slowly back and forth on his chair in pursuit of the most lifelike image from the photographs now spread out on the blotter. "And maybe it won't," came the glum conclusion as the chair rocked down with a thud. "See one bloke all blurred in a balaclava helmet and you've seen the lot." The bulldog gnashed his teeth in sheer frustration. "*Two days*—television coverage, for heaven's sake—and there hasn't been a soul phoned in to say they recognised anything about the blighters that could help nail 'em—no distinctive walk, no characteristic way of gunning an engine or taking a corner on two wheels . . ."

He glowered at Stone as if he held her personally to blame for this. "*We* didn't recognise anything, either." He took a deep breath. "But *they're* supposed to be experts. Hah damnation hah! Focus. Alignment. Direction. Light, shade, contrast . . ." As he parroted the excuses and provisos of the forensic lab's report, his fist thumped bitterly on the bulkiest folder of the depressing assortment on his desk. "And then," he snarled, "when they feed the M.O. into their perishing computer, it prints a list so long we might as well turn it straight into toilet paper for all the good it'll do."

Stone opened her mouth to point out that the technology was only as good as those who programmed it, then shut it quickly as he glowered at her again.

"Well—so much for the boffins." He stopped glowering to roll his eyes in despair to the ceiling. "Just our luck. Even if the Pearce crowd had been filming smack inside the bank and got the blighters' voices, through that blasted nylon fuzz they would've been so distorted their own mothers would never have known them." His gaze came down from the faded distemper overhead to fasten once more, accusingly, upon the desktop folders. "*Enhanced* or not. What we want is some good old-fashioned stand-up-in-court evidence, not this scientific jiggery-pokery that lives in hope. We want *fingerprints*. We want . . . We want . . ."

He began waving his glasses helplessly in the air.

"We want," supplied Stone, "an informer or two to come out of the woodwork. E. M. Forster, for instance."

The helpless gesturing gave way to a wry grimace. "Forster's a wily old devil," the superintendent conceded.

"He knows his job. If he's after a scoop, he isn't going to give anything away unless he wants to—not even to us." The bloodhound gloom lightened into an unexpected grin. "Remind me to tell you some time about how I tried to get him loosened up over a few beers. Just after he got back from seeing how he liked the Fleet Street experience, that would have been. Long before your time."

"Tried," echoed Stone, her eyes beginning to dance as she saw his expression change. "And . . . a *few* beers?"

"Don't remind me!" In the interests of professional dignity he decided to turn the conversation. "I've often wondered if he really came back because he didn't think much of Fleet Street, or whether it was because Fleet Street was too much for him. Big fish, small pond . . . It's got a lot going for it. And Forster has a pretty strong sense of self-preservation. Even his liver," he added. "*Especially* his liver."

Stone was matter-of-fact about her superior's evident but long-past suffering. "Then as you say, sir, Forster knows his job. Knows how to look after himself." She frowned at the witness statement she had just removed from its cardboard file. "And a good thing, too, if he's going after an exclusive on the bank robbers. They've been successful once—"

"Once?" barked the superintendent, thumping the computer printout in its accusing folder.

"They have been successful," Stone reiterated firmly. "So they're bound to try again, sooner or later. Success in crime might be said to, um, breed excess, sir."

"They don't know when to stop," translated Trewley. "Idiots, the lot of 'em."

"Yes, sir. Which means we'll stand a better chance of catching them if—when—they repeat themselves . . . But it also means that if Forster starts poking about and learns too much, it might be dangerous. Don't you think we should try talking to him—persuade him to talk to us—for his own sake as well as ours?"

"He won't talk if he doesn't want to," Trewley insisted. "But you needn't worry about E. M. Forster, Stone. The man can look after himself. You have my personal guarantee!"

•   •   •

OF THE SEVEN days of the drinking week, the three busiest of Allingham's alcoholic calendar were Wednesday, Friday, and Saturday. Each Wednesday, the pubs were packed with market traders drinking their profits or, on very rare occasions, drowning their sorrows. On Friday and Saturday it was the turn of roistering youth to displace all but the hardiest of the older generation whose claim to the most comfortable seats and the barmaids' best attentions was understood by everyone concerned to be limited to the other four days of the week.

Fleet Street reporters, even those in exile, must be hardy. If they weaken, they go under. E. M. Forster, exile though he was, had no intention of going under in either the metaphorical or the literal sense. It was a brave roisterer who would attempt to chivvy Forster off his favourite chair or to jog his elbow at the bar. It was, as Trewley had found, not so much a brave as a foolhardy reveller who would try to keep up with him when he was drinking. *Going under* in the literal sense might be a reference to tables, but it did not refer to E. M. Forster.

"Same again, please." The voice of the lean, grey man in the tweed jacket was only slightly muzzy with beer and smoke as he reached out to push his empty glass in the direction of the smiling barmaid. Tracy leaned over and swept it up to add to the collection on her crowded tray. She hadn't caught his words—there was far too much noise in the bar tonight for that—but he was a regular customer. She knew by instinct what he'd said, and nodded cheerfully at him.

"Don't blame you for celebrating," she cried above the hubbub that was louder than she could ever remember for a Friday. Everyone was busy talking about the bank robbery, and whistles were being wetted at twice the usual rate. "Must be nice to have been right on the spot when it happened, and to get such a good story—coo!" The tips were coming twice as fast, too. "Bet they paid you double this week for a story like that!"

"Oh?" said Forster, arching a sardonic eyebrow. Tracy

giggled. Once again she hadn't heard what he'd said, but she could tell from the look of him that she was meant to find it funny, so like a good barmaid she did. The customer was always right unless he was paralytic—and nobody in living memory had ever seen E. M. Forster that much the worse for drink. "I'll get your order," she cried, and coughed with the effort of shouting.

A masculine voice more easily penetrated the smoky commotion. "Saw your piece in the *Argus*, Mr. Forster." Tracy, coughing and giggling by turns, had filled her tray with empties and was hurrying back to the bar. A thin young man wearing a leather jacket studded with so much metal that he walked with a stoop had materialised in her place. He had a young woman—Forster peered through the smoke and corrected his first impression—a young*ish* woman on his arm, plumply curved and brassy-haired, with rather too much makeup that did nothing for her undoubtedly remarkable blue eyes.

"Ah," said E. M. Forster. "Yes. Of course."

The stooped and studded young man shot a look of triumph at the brassy, shapely, blue-eyed blonde. "The front page," he said. "Clever stuff. Make your name, eh?"

"Ah-ha," said E. M. Forster, and arched another eyebrow.

"Famous, yeah?" the studded one explained, in case the excitement and everything had been too much for the poor old devil after all. "Told her I knew you," he went on, digging his companion cheerily in the ribs. She winced but did not move away.

Forster contemplated the thin, pale face above the black leather without speaking, as a scientist will study a rare specimen under the microscope. "Knew who you were," amended Leather Jacket, after an uneasy pause.

Even this evident backtracking did not deter the plump and comely, over-made-up blonde, who beamed a smile in the reporter's direction and waited for the customary invitation to join him.

E. M. Forster frowned, peering again through the smoke and even taking the cigarette from his mouth to clear the air. Shrewd blue eyes met his gaze for the briefest of moments, then wavered and fell as the young woman pressed closer to the leather jacket and favoured its wearer with another dazzling smile.

"Wants to meet you," said Leather Jacket, emboldened by the gesture. "Told her I could introduce you."

E. M. Forster inclined his head. "And so you can," was all he said. His quick frown had been replaced by the vain and vacant smile of one who knows he does his little world a favour by being a celebrity. "Sit down . . . , my dear." The role of celebrity was not easy to learn.

After an adroit spot of furniture-shuffling the youngish (in her thirties, thought Forster on closer inspection) woman found herself sitting in the corner beside the reporter, with Leather Jacket, somehow, still standing. "Ah. Thank you," came the polite dismissal from the older man. Leather Jacket, with a mumbled appeal ignored by the young woman, shrugged his studded shoulders and headed back to the bar.

"There, now," said the plump young blonde, sounding more than pleased. "Alone at last." She giggled.

"In a manner of speaking." The reporter glanced across to where Leather Jacket stood brooding over a drink at the bar on the edge of a chattering crowd.

The blonde giggled. "Oh, it's much more private in a pub where everybody's talking at once. Who's got time to listen to anyone else?"

"You . . . may have a point." He tried not to sound surprised: Celebrities were supposedly accustomed to any amount of idiocy from those wanting to meet them, and he ought to play the celebrity game. "E. M. Forster," he introduced himself with a sketchy bow. "No relation," he added out of habit, though he doubted she would understand.

The blonde smiled. "Sherry," she said. As—despite his celebrity, Forster raised a sceptical eyebrow—she giggled again. "Russell," she added. "It's my name: Sheri Russell." And she spelled it, letter by letter. "I'm very pleased to meet you, Mr. Forster."

"Why?" The mantle of celebrity was wearisome. He

could afford to relax, to be blunt, now that she was sitting down.

Sheri blinked, then rallied. "Well, I don't know any reporters, not personally I mean, and you're ever so famous, they say."

"Indeed." He achieved a faint smile. "Allow me to buy you a drink." The smile grew wider. "Sweet?"

"Ooh yes, please," said Sheri. The gleam in Forster's eye was swiftly suppressed. He wondered whether Leather Jacket—still at the bar, still drinking—had noticed what was going on.

Barmaid Tracy was heading past with her umpteenth tray of empties. E. M. Forster hailed her. "One double vodka, one sweet sherry, please. A schooner."

Tracy looked startled, but recalled that the customer was always right. "When I've dumped these, Mr. Forster."

"Thank you," said Sheri Russell, breathless with gratitude as Tracy hurried away. "I *knew* you must be famous. I mean—only top-notch reporters get paid enough to be able to buy people drinks, don't they?"

"Ah," came the gnomic response.

"You'll have done well, out of writing up that robbery, I expect. Sell it to the national papers, too, did you? Being an eyewitness and all, I mean."

"Only doing my job," replied E. M. Forster.

"It must be ever so interesting. I've often thought I'd like to be a reporter. You know, always in the middle of things, and knowing secrets before they happen, and telling the world what you see and hear, and having everyone know who you are, the way they do with you."

"Takes time," Forster told her. "And effort. Hard work—and luck," he added.

"Being in the right place at the right time." Sheri nodded. "I mean, you couldn't have known they were going to rob that bank, could you?" Blue eyes widened in a look of gleeful horror. "Ooh, you didn't know, did you?"

"Not much gets past—that is, no. I didn't." He'd better watch his tongue. Back to the modest celebrity act until his opportunity came. "Sometimes you make your own luck, my dear, and this was one of those happy occasions."

"How thrilling! You'll be writing it all up properly in next week's paper, I suppose. Personal details to make it, well, more real. Local interest and stuff."

"A front page spread," he assured her gravely as Tracy approached with the drinks.

"Cheers—and thanks." Sheri raised her glass and gave him a roguish smile over the rim as she sipped.

E. M. Forster inclined his head as he, too, drank. "So you fancy yourself as a reporter, do you?" he said, trying to keep the sceptical note out of his voice.

"I've always thought it must be so interesting." Her eyelashes were rich black sweeps of seduction above cerulean blue. "Do tell me about it."

"Your friend might prefer it if I didn't."

"My friend?"

"Might not like it if I monopolise you."

"Oh. Yes." Sheri followed the direction of his gaze and turned to where Leather Jacket stood brooding over another pint of beer as he watched them from beneath a furrowed brow. "Him. Oh, he won't mind." Sheri sounded very sure of herself.

She might have sounded less sure if she had spotted the reporter tipping half his vodka quickly into her glass, but she didn't. When she turned back, Forster was sitting just as he had sat before. "Tell me." His smile might have warned her, but it didn't. "My dear. In what particular aspect of the journalistic life are you . . . particularly . . . interested?" enquired E. M. Forster.

"Oh. Everything, really." This was too much for him. She saw his eyebrows arch. "I mean," she said with one of her quick giggles, "how you find your stories—and how you manage to be on the spot when things happen—and how you add the human interest to something, oh, like that bank raid when that sort of thing happens all over the place and you have to make it different. *You* know."

"Drink up," said E. M. Forster. "I rather think I do."

Seven

"TIME, GENTLEMEN, PLEASE!" is the traditional prepare-to-be-chucked-out call of England's pubs, traditionally called at ten-thirty each night of the week from Monday until Thursday. On Friday and Saturday landlords allow their customers an extra half an hour before Last Orders, together with the customary fifteen minutes for the emptying of any glasses that might only just have been filled. It is therefore closer to midnight than to eleven on Fridays and Saturdays when people ejected from public houses find themselves anything like close to home, even in so relatively small a town as Allingham.

It was well after midnight when a group of young men, hoarse from hurling insults and chanting football slogans at their favourite antagonists until both sides were tired, swaggered and weaved and sang their boastful way down a narrow alley that debouched into the concrete forecourt of an elderly block of flats dwarfed by the modern semi-monstrosity in which most of the young men lived.

Tattered clouds darkened the gibbous moon and turned harmless shadows into flickering menace as its pewter gleam briefly appeared, then vanished, then reappeared only to vanish again. The lamp standard at the far end of the alley had a broken bulb.

The young men did not realise this until it was too late to turn back from the encroaching dark. None of them would have dared to lose face by suggesting they went round the long way, so everyone huddled closer together without seeming to, swaggering and chanting and singing all the more as they drew farther from the light at the street end of the alley into narrow, high-walled, smothering blackness. They tried to care nothing for the uncomfortable fact that their already tiny band had been reduced in size by one with the early homeward desertion of a youth in a brooding temper the very instant the pub clock chimed the hour.

"Roll me over," bawled the young men, "in the clover! Roll me over, lay me down, and do it—"

"Oof!"

"Ugh!"

"Watch where you're bloody well going!"

The leader of the gang, arm-in-arm with his lieutenant, had stumbled over something lying in the deepest part of the shadows. His cohorts, close behind, stood no chance.

"Bloody great feet," grumbled someone as he picked himself up.

"Bloody hard elbows," offered someone else, dusting himself down.

"Bloody hell!" The gang leader's voice was a breathless squeak, and not just because he had been at the bottom of the cascade of bodies. Still kneeling on the ground, he cleared his throat and tried again. "This here what we fell over," he brought out as his henchmen sorted themselves out. "It—it ain't just a bundle of rags . . ."

"Bloody hell," echoed his second-in-command, groping in the dark as his eyes became accustomed. "It's . . . a body."

"A bloke," enlarged the leader, braver now the word had been uttered. "And I reckon he ain't so dead, neither. Not—not cold, anyhow."

"His head's all . . . sticky," said the second-in-command, and fell silent.

"Then we'd best get him out of here," someone said after a moment.

"We'd best get *us* out of here," amended someone else above a tentative observation that you weren't meant to move people who were unconscious in case you made things worse. "Shut up, Jerry. He's been mugged, right? So who's going to get the blame? The ones what found him. They'll say we only pretended to find him. They'll say—"

"Leave it out, Darren." The leader spoke with scorn at his colleague's panic. "It won't be us they blame *because* we're the ones what found him, see? Use yer loaf. We've all bin together the whole evening, we can prove it if they ask—and it can't have happened that long ago or . . ."

There was another pause.

"Or . . . someone else would've found him before we did," supplied the second lieutenant.

There came the longest silence yet.

"Can't be helped," came the reluctant conclusion of the gang leader. "Duffing up the other team what's able to take care of themselves is one thing, but bashing old geezers over the head's a bit much. If you lot want to nip off home and—tell anyone what's happened, that your business. *I* say we tell the ambulance. If we don't," he added above the murmur of peer group solidarity, "and this here bloke dies, then that's *murder*. With us accessories. Look good on the files, won't it?"

Children of the media generation, they knew at once what he meant. Tabloid newspapers and television documentaries regularly warned not only that Big Brother was watching, but also that he was feeding detailed notes of what he watched into his omnipotent computer. The Government kept files; the police, the Social Services, the tax man kept files. The hands that worked the keyboard ruled the world.

"We'll go and phone, then." The leader rose to his feet and squinted down the alleyway. In the distance the lighter darkness of the concrete forecourt was a reassuring sight. "Some of us, I mean. Because someone'll have to stay here. Stop anyone else tripping over him and . . . making it worse." The words echoed in his memory, and he brightened. "Hey, Bennett. You game?"

Jerry Bennett sighed. He had brought it on himself, he supposed. "Yeah, all right. But make it quick."

"Darren'll keep you company." The statement was spoken as an order. Jerry stifled another sigh. Darren groaned under his breath, but said nothing aloud. The two young men stood together in silence and watched their colleagues hurry away. Nobody was singing or swaggering now.

EVEN THIS LATE in the twentieth century there are many in Britain who, lacking cars, rely on public transport, on the kindness of neighbours, or (weather permitting) on Shanks's Pony to travel from A to B. Some travellers hold strong views on conservation, pollution, and the current vogue for Greenery; others are just plain stingy. Cars and their upkeep cost money.

For all the above and for others of like mind, there is no disguising the blessings bestowed by the corner shop. Every parish worthy of the name has its cluster of small stores that ease the burden of local consumers who, for whatever reason, dislike having to journey too far from home to find what they want in the way of life's essentials. Within the space of a hundred yards or so one might find a newsagent and stationer, a pharmacy, a grocer (green and/or general), and a baker—none of whom are part of any national chain—cheerfully rubbing shoulders with a sub-post office, a travel agent, a butcher, a florist, and perhaps a dentist's surgery as well.

When the funeral parlour moved to larger premises closer to the middle of town, Eye Deal Opticians took over the lease. The firm, established for only four years, had in that time built up an excellent reputation for sharpness of price, quality of service, and the cheery smile all who crossed the threshold were guaranteed to receive. Karen Crabtree was a native of Allingham, but would have greeted a stranger with as much warmth as she did a client who had known her in her cradle: That was the sort of person she was. It was nothing to do with the fact that Eye Deal was a one-woman business and hoped to expand: Mrs. Crabtree had been born smiling.

In a one-woman business it is, of course, impossible to keep a permanent watch for customers. Karen had suspended above the lintel a set of homemade pottery bells with metal clappers that sounded a loud, unmelodious alarm

when anyone opened the door. This was cheaper than
anything electric, and less likely to fuse if the rain came in
through the roof, which needed retiling.

Karen was in the back boiling the kettle for her first cup
of the day when the clanking carillon rang out. She put
down the milk, glanced through the one-way mirror in the
wall, recognised a stranger, and hurried out to welcome her.

"Good morning," she said with a smile.

"Morning." The stranger—plump but shapely, in her
thirties, with brilliant blue eyes even an excessive use of
cosmetics could not dim—nodded vaguely as she gazed
about the room. "Yes . . ."

Karen wondered what she made of the secondhand filing
cabinets (they had been refurbished, but the contractor
couldn't work miracles) with the fish tank on top, and the
aspidistra (which stayed green without requiring too much
cossetting). She seemed to be paying more attention to them
than to the rows of frames and the display of assorted
spectacle cases on the opposite wall.

"Yes," said the woman again, just as Mrs. Crabtree was
about to ask if she was looking for anything in particular.
"Um—contact lenses. I mean, cleaner. Do you sell it?"

"Oh, yes." Mrs. Crabtree, forebearing to add that she
could supply the lenses, too, waved in the direction of a set
of shelves that filled an awkward corner. The blue gaze
followed the gesture without seeming to see. "Hard, soft, or
disposable?"

"Pardon?"

"The contacts. You can have a different sort of cleaner for
each type. What brand do you usually buy?"

"Oh," said the plump woman, blinking. "Um—the cheap-
est, I suppose. I mean," she enlarged as Karen tried not to look
puzzled. "It isn't for me, you know." She giggled. "Silly me.
There's no reason why you should, is there? Know, I mean.
But . . . um, I don't wear contacts myself, and I'm not sure
what sort my friend's got. The . . . um, usual sort, I think."
She pursed her scarlet lips and frowned. Then she nodded.
"Yes, I'm sure of it."

"The hard sort you take out every night?" Karen wanted to be sure, too.

"Yes," said the plump woman firmly.

"Not soft? Not disposable?" persisted the optician.

"The ordinary hard sort," said the woman a little irritably. "What can you recommend for cleaning them?"

Karen waved once more towards the shelves. A display of small shock-orange cardboard stars with black price figures in the centre ran down the wall side of the fixture. "All these are good," she said, "but we're doing a special offer on Hyaline brand this week and next. Ten percent reduction if you buy two."

"I'll just take one," said the woman, licking her lips. "The smallest size," she added, and Karen took it from the shelf and showed it to her.

"Yes," said the woman again, sounding relieved. "Yes, that'll do. I'll take it. Thanks."

And, after handing over the money, she took the bottle and was gone.

"JEANS!" DETECTIVE SUPERINTENDENT Trewley let out a sudden bulldog roar that had the pens and pencils dancing in the old marmalade jar on his desk. "How many people wear the blasted things, for heaven's sake?"

He'd been snorting over the forensic reports ever since he read the first paragraph of the first, and this last intelligence appeared to be the final straw. For a Saturday morning, his mood did not bode well for the rest of the weekend. Stone, working overtime with what had, when she left home, been a relatively light heart, sighed. She herself was wearing jeans that day, but she knew that this was not what had upset him.

"Half the population of the country, I should think," she returned firmly. He might as well have something worth brooding about. "If not more."

"That's not funny, Stone."

"Maybe not, sir, but it's, um, realistic. Everybody under thirty wears jeans for casual as a matter of course." She glanced down at her own neat, restrained curves in their blue denim covering. "And manufacturers have realised that people who, um, grew up wearing jeans for casual don't want to stop now that they're . . . maturing. So they're cutting them on more generous lines to suit the—fuller figure, and absolutely everybody's buying them now." There was a twinkle in her eye as she delivered the punch line. "With obvious exceptions, naturally."

"I wouldn't wear jeans if I—if I lost three stone," retorted Trewley, who was feeling guilty about the diet he had been so quick to abandon after the Allshire and National holdup. "A pair of old cords suits me fine."

"Ah." The twinkle grew brighter. "If you distinguish between cord and denim jeans, then I'd say lots of people feel the same as you do. And if it wasn't a rhetorical question, but was inspired by the fibres found in the car, I'd say denim would narrow it down to, oh, well under half the population, sir. Say forty percent as opposed to . . ." She frowned. "Fifty-five."

"Thank you, Stone."

She ignored the ominous note in his voice as she began warming to her process of elimination. "So, forty percent— and they're not all blue, nowadays. Ten percent will be black, grey, khaki . . . Say thirty percent, sir."

"Thirty percent," rumbled the bulldog obediently, with the hint of a smile now starting to soften the harsh creases of his face.

Stone was settling comfortably into her stride. "About five percent of those will be the sort with elastic to help them keep their shape, so if the fibres we're interested in are plain, we're down to twenty-five . . . and there are, let's see, half a dozen major manufacturers? All using their own particular fibres and dyes and dyeing methods. Forensic have a list of the most likely—"

The telephone rang. Stone became serious at once. As the superintendent picked up his receiver, she prepared to eavesdrop on the other line if instructed.

"Trewley," Trewley told the mouthpiece. His voice changed. "The hospital?"

Stone hesitated for only a few seconds before snatching

up her own phone. Superintendent Trewley might have a wife and daughters as hostages to fortune, but he was not alone.

". . . concussion," the hospital was saying as the sergeant put the telephone to her ear. "And a hairline fracture of the skull. He's unconscious, of course. Heaven only knows when he'll come round again."

Stone felt a cold fluttering in her midriff. A male rather than a female victim: The superintendent was off the hook. But . . .

"Well, he's in the right place," said Trewley. His eyes met those of Stone—begging him in a silence she could not bring herself to break to tell her the worst—and did their best to telegraph reassurance. As his features at the best of times were hardly reassuring, the attempt only served to confuse her. "Concussion can be nasty."

"With mild exposure on top of it," the telephone told him. "From lying out half the night before he was found." Stone stifled a sigh of quiet relief. There had been no time the previous night when she had been alone. "Let's hope he doesn't end up with a chest infection," the telephone concluded. "Not your problem, of course, but your desk sergeant thought you ought to know."

"Yes," said Trewley. "Yes. Thanks." Deeper furrows formed on his already corrugated brow. "We'll be in touch," he told the telephone after a pause. "Might even send a bloke to keep an eye on him. Yes. Don't let any visitors in until you've heard from us, will you?"

"We won't," promised the telephone, and broke the connection. Trewley dropped his receiver on its cradle, and turned to Stone with a grim expression in his eyes.

"How much of that did you get? Once you stopped worrying about Young What's-His-Name, I mean?"

"A man's in hospital—probably after having been hit on the head—but I couldn't work out who it was," she said. "Someone Sergeant Pleate thinks is important—which isn't to say every assault isn't important, because it is, but normally he'd just put it on the sheet, and we'd hear about it in a routine report."

"So?" prompted Trewley, as she paused. "You're supposed to be a detective, girl. Use your powers of deduction."

"And inference," she appended quickly. "Um. A chap wearing jeans that match the fibres—except that Pleate hasn't read the Forensic stuff as far as I know, so he'd have no reason to tell us especially. Or . . ." She watched Trewley pick up a pen and tap his blotter with it. "Well, our most important case at present is the bank robbery," she went on. "But it can't be anyone who's already in hospital. None of them was well enough, the last I heard, to be discharged, so how did he manage to lie outside half the night? No." She looked suddenly pleased with herself. "One of the film crew? One of the witnesses, anyway."

He nodded. "And what you might call a high profile witness, at that. Piers Perishing Pearce might've got his name in lights all over the country, but here in Allshire we've a star of our own. It may be only coincidence." His tone was grave. "I hope it is—and you know how I hate the blasted things—but we can't afford to take the risk that it isn't. He makes a big splash on the front page of yesterday's paper with how he saw the holdup start to finish, and that very night someone whacks him over the head in an alleyway with a length of two-by-four or a blasted brick." Trewley wagged a forefinger in his sergeant's direction. "I *don't* like coincidence, Stone."

"I know," she murmured.

"No," he echoed her. "I don't. So I'll risk a sizeable bet that somebody not a million miles away from the Allshire and National affair has got it in for E. M. Forster . . ."

"No takers, sir," said Detective Sergeant Stone.

Eight

IF EYE DEAL'S Karen wanted an inspiration to succeed, she need look no further than the example of Thomas Hobson. Born, like Mrs. Crabtree, in Allingham, this optician of an earlier generation had begun with just one shop at the far end of a side street near the market. Now there were seven branches of Hobson's Choice dotted about Allshire, with the smallest—Hobson was a sentimental man—the original premises in the county town.

Day-to-day management of the chain had recently been handed to Hobson's grandson, another Thomas. Young Tom had gone to business school and knew far more about Efficiency and Image than he did about the dispensing of spectacles and contact lenses, which he wisely left to the experts in the firm's employ. He took out a loan with the Allshire and National Bank to instal new, bulk-purchased carpets, antitilt filing cabinets—part of his course had included Health and Safety in the Workplace—and desktop computers in each of the seven shops. He streamlined the allocation of spectacle frames to different areas (glitter went well on the coast, farmers preferred tortoiseshell, sophisticated smoky shades sold best in towns) and found a wholesaler to offer more favourable terms on the most up-to-date styles.

Favourable terms or not, there was still a good deal of capital tied up in the spectacle frames. Tom's next logical step was to insist that all the old-fashioned doorbells must be replaced by electric buzzers activated by a beam of light and a magic eye. Whenever the beam was broken by movement, the buzzer would sound the alarm. On market days and Saturdays the constant alarming as people popped in and out drove the workforce wild, but nobody could deny that the amount of petty pilfering—orange guard-chains for the absentminded, magnifying glasses, fancy spectacle cases of tapestry or suede—had been much reduced since the buzzers had been inflicted on the seven Hobson shops.

The buzzer went. Customers in the shop winced, but the workforce had gone beyond exasperation into selective deafness. "Let me bend this earpiece round a little more for you," said a helpful youth with a charming smile to a balding man with a beard.

"Now, you just look at yourself in the mirror to see how you like the fit," said a matronly woman to another matron as tweedily dressed as herself. "And the shape. They really suit you, if you want my honest opinion . . ."

From around a corner emerged a tall elderly man in gold-rimmed glasses and a white coat. He was escorting a mother and a nervous-looking small child who rubbed the bridge of her freckled nose in a marked manner. "Bring her back in six months to be on the safe side," said the tall elderly man. "But I'm sure there's no need for you to worry. The school doctors know what they're doing."

"Oh, thank you, Mr. Paine." The mother smiled; her offspring, after a surreptitious poke in the shoulder blades, piped her own courteous thanks and then dragged her mother by the hand towards the door before Mr. Paine could change his mind and make her wear those horrid heavy metal frame things with the click-click lenses again.

The little girl moved with a surprising turn of speed. She and her mother had to swerve to avoid the stranger who had just entered and now stood in the middle of the floor: a plump woman, shapely, in her thirties, with brilliant blue eyes that darted about the busy space as if determined not to miss a single one of young Tom Hobson's improvements.

"Ah," said Mr. Paine, observing that his staff were

otherwise occupied. "Excuse me, but are you looking for anything in particular? How may I help you?"

"Contact lens cleaner," said the plump woman, still contemplating the various fixtures and fittings around the room. "The hard sort," she added. "Please."

The optician nodded to a middle-aged woman waiting on one of the chairs by the door. "I'll be with you in a moment, Mrs. Prendergast!" he told her. Then, turning back to the newcomer, he went on: "Contact lens cleaner? Certainly. Which brand do you prefer?"

The woman's blue eyes shifted from Mr. Paine's quiet grey regard. "Hyaline," she said after a moment. "Please."

"An excellent choice," said Mr. Paine. His gold rims glittered as he nodded his approval. "And which size would you prefer?"

Again that shift of attention. "Small. Please."

"The economy size works out cheaper per unit price," volunteered Mr. Paine politely.

"I'm—we're here on holiday," said the plump woman as if this explained her choice.

As indeed it did. "I hope you have an enjoyable stay," said Mr. Paine as he took a plastic bottle from the shelf behind the counter, wrapped it in a paper bag, rang up the price on the till, and accepted a ten-pound note in payment. It was habit rather than deliberate discourtesy that made him check that the authentic metal strip showed as it was meant to do: dotted on one side, invisible on the other, and solid when held against the light. Mr. Paine counted out her change, and the plump woman left.

After she had gone, he couldn't decide whether she had seemed more affronted or perturbed by his action. He would like to have assured her that every treasury note tendered in a Hobson shop was automatically treated with the same degree of suspicion, but labouring the point in this way would only have made matters worse.

Oh, well. Mentally, Mr. Paine shrugged. "If you'd like to come this way, Mrs. Prendergast," he called to his next appointment, and led the way back around the corner of his consulting room.

He spared no more thought for the plump, shapely, blue-eyed woman: out of sight, out of mind. And why not?

People bought contact lens cleaner all the time.

CONSTABLE BENSON BRUSHED a few specks of dust from the peak of his cap, then replaced the cap on his head and adjusted it in his driving mirror to the correct angle. Approachable, but undoubtedly competent. Some of the nurses at Allingham General were such snobs they couldn't see that anyone except a doctor was worth dating.

Striding manfully from the panda car to the hospital's main entrance, Benson spared a few moments to wonder what sort of doctor Detective Sergeant Stone would have made, then checked the shine on his uniform buttons and squared his shoulders as he pushed open the swing doors and headed for Reception.

"You've got a Mr. Forster here," he said to the battle-axe behind the desk, who was younger than he'd expected—now that he looked closely, no older than he was—but who seemed to have the regulation glare down to a fine art. "Brought in last night. Suspected mugging."

"I must check my records." The battle-axe pursed her lips. "How do you spell it? The name sounds familiar."

Carefully Benson spelled it. "Writes for the *Argus*," he added. "Had a big piece on the front page yesterday."

"Oh. One moment." She turned aside to address herself to her computer. As her slim, rose-tipped fingers danced over the keyboard, she frowned at Benson, who had instinctively leaned over the desk to look at the screen.

"Ahem!" came the warning cough. Benson blushed. "These records," he was told, "are confidential. Personal. Police or not—ah, yes, here we are. This morning."

"What?"

"He was admitted this morning, not last night. The ambulance delivered him at twenty past twelve . . ." As she studied the screen, her voice tailed away. "Is this visit authorised?"

"Here's my identification." Benson had hoped that the

sight of him in his uniform would have been enough, and felt rather deflated as he produced his leather wallet.

"This could be forged." The battle-axe tried to sound threatening.

"I came in a panda car. It's parked outside."

"You could have stolen it." Was that a faint smile curving the corners of her mouth?

"You could ring the station. Ask them to describe me."

Yes: a definite smile. "Let me see your identification again." She gave the photograph a long, thoughtful look before turning to the written details. "So that's you, is it? Name, rank, and number, you might say. Full name, too."

"My friends," volunteered Benson, "call me—"

"Not in working hours I'm sure they don't."

"There's always after hours," ventured Benson.

"So there is." Why had he ever thought her a battle-axe? "I'm lucky to work regular hours. Nine to five." Her smile was teasing. "Not like you. All that overtime."

"In the public interest," said Police Constable Benson, his chest swelling. "Flexible, though. A day or so extra here and there soon adds up."

"You can tell me about it once you've been to check on Mr. Forster." She was serious now. "It says here . . . well, I had to be careful, you know."

"I know. And *you* know he'll be okay with me there to keep an eye on him."

She answered the unspoken question. "Pasteur Ward, down that corridor and fourth on the left. I'll let them know you're coming."

"Perhaps I'll see you when I'm going."

"Perhaps. If you've left your car in a reserved space, I'll see you sooner than that."

"Promises, promises." Benson snapped off a crisp salute and grinned. The battle-axe grinned back. "Nine to five," he said as he turned towards the corridor. "Every day?"

"Every day," he was assured.

His lighthearted mood fell away as he pushed open the rubber doors of Pasteur Ward to have his nostrils assailed by the pungent floral smell of disinfectant. It would be even worse in Intensive Care, he supposed.

A sudden harsh grating made him jump and look round.

"Yes?" The question came from a female head crowned with a starched white frill that had popped through an open glass hatch. "We really must get that seen to," the head added in an irritable aside. "Visiting hours aren't until after lunch. Wait there."

Obediently Benson waited. Quick footsteps heralded the approach of the whole body, which proved to be trim, navy-blue clad, and adorned by a white apron topped by a black elastic belt with an elaborate silver buckle. "I'm Sister," said Sister. No other identification was necessary. "And who are you?"

Benson produced his wallet. Sister nodded. "Ah, yes, I see. And who do *you* want to see?"

"Mr. Forster from the *Argus*. I thought you knew."

Sister favoured him with a steady look. "Oh, we knew. I thought *you* knew we had to be careful. Someone from the police station phoned about it less than an hour ago." She paused and looked at him again.

"That'd be Superintendent Trewley," said Benson. "Or perhaps Sergeant Stone," he added as she hesitated. "She knows all about medical things, see, on account of training for a doctor before she joined the force."

Sister smiled. "We had quite a chat," she said. "The sergeant is as surprised—and pleased—as we are that Mr. Forster seems to be on the way to a remarkable recovery. He started to come round not long after we first spoke to the police about his admission. You might even be able to talk to him, though he may not make much sense."

"I thought he was out cold." Benson fell into step behind her as she beckoned him towards a side room at the end of the entrance lobby.

"He may have slipped again, so don't try to wake him if he has." She lowered her voice as she led Benson into the little room. "Mr. Forster?"

The window blinds were half down, casting a restful green light over the long, lean figure under the counterpane of the gunmetal grey hospital bed. A white crepe bandage, bulky with gauze and lint, was around the figure's head. A thin tube depending from a transparent plastic bag at the top of a tall stand was stuck with a strip of plaster to the figure's left arm.

"He's gone again," murmured Sister. "You can sit there until he wakes. Don't make a noise."

Benson had never been made so conscious of the way his boots squeaked as when Sister drew in her breath to hear him tiptoe across the polished linoleum to the chair at the head of E. M. Forster's bed.

"Quiet!" she hissed as, blushing, he took his seat. "I'll send someone in with a cup of tea for you," she added, taking some pity on his embarrassment. "Do try not to drop it and disturb the patient."

On this Parthian shot, she bustled out. "Rather have whisky," came a croak from the bed as Benson watched her go. "Or beer. Tea? Ugh."

"Mr. Forster!" Benson realised that he was croaking in sympathy. He cleared his throat and achieved a moderate whisper. "Mr. Forster . . . how do you feel?"

"Head hurts." The reporter opened his eyes. "Ugh." He closed them again.

"Are you up to talking? To telling me what happened," Benson quickly amended. Forster's eyelids flickered, but he said nothing for some moments. Benson saw the counterpane rise and fall, rise and fall with a slow, steady rhythm.

"Chatted up," said Forster at last, still without opening his eyes.

Benson felt himself blush and was thankful the reporter could not see him. But—how had he known? Had the injury to his head made him—psychic?

"Rubbish," muttered Benson sturdily.

"Life in the old dog yet." Forster blinked indignantly at the young constable, who didn't know what to say. "Knew she was up to something," said E. M. Forster. "Not a fool."

"Er," said Benson. "Well . . . no." It was about as noncommittal as he could get. He was starting to wonder what they were really discussing.

"N—ugh." The reporter had tried to nod his approval of the sentiment expressed, and the movement made him wince. "Head hurts," he said again. "Dammit."

"Oh," came a fresh young female voice from the doorway. "You're awake, Mr. Forster!"

The reporter's eyes flew open. "I know!" he snapped at the nurse who was coming towards the bed with a cup of tea in her hand. "Wide awake," he enlarged, as she hesitated. "That for me?"

"Yes," said Benson as the nurse still hesitated. This unexpected intervention made her take two steps back.

"Not until Doctor says so," she said, preparing for further retreat. "You've had a nasty bump on the head, and you mustn't try to hurry your recovery. You need to rest."

"Slops," said E. M. Forster. The degree of scorn he was able to inject into one sibilant syllable was remarkable. "Tubes!" He turned his head on the pillow to glare at the innocent life-giving drip in his arm. He turned back to see Benson trying to smother a grin. "Go and find a doctor for me, there's a good girl," said E. M. Forster.

It was the wordsmith's first complete sentence, and it seemed to do him good. "Go on!" he commanded, pushing himself up on his pillows, ignoring the nurse's shocked dismay. "I've had enough of this." He turned back to Benson. "If a man isn't even allowed a cup of tea in this place, it's high time I got out of here."

"I only said," said the nurse, "that it's not my responsibility to let you have anything by mouth until Doctor says you can—"

"Then fetch him," snarled E. M. Forster. The nurse, with one horrified backward look at the rebel with the bandaged head, fled the room and could be heard pattering down the entrance lobby the way she had come.

"Ugh." The reporter subsided again. "Monstrous regimen. Give anything for a whisky." He looked hopefully at Benson. "Not on duty, I suppose."

"That's right, sir." Benson had some sympathy for the implied request, but he was well aware that victims of concussion should on no account be given alcohol, even a man like Forster, who seemed surprisingly on the ball.

"Fleet Street was never this tough," said the reporter with a shaky laugh. "Just grin and bear it, then, I won't even bother asking anyone if I'm allowed to have a cigarette." He put his free hand gingerly to the bandage round his head. "It looks worse than it is, I dare say."

"You certainly seem to have had a—a bit of a bump," observed Benson.

E. M. Forster almost laughed, but the stiffness of his facial muscles stopped him. "Tactful," he said, wincing. "You don't care to venture an opinion on the severity of said bump—but I suppose I can't blame you."

"I'm no doctor, sir. Basic first-aid training's all we get in the police."

"The police. Yes." The reporter's instincts had never entirely deserted him. "This isn't just a social call, of course. You want to know what I remember about last night." He favoured Benson with a shrewd glance. "Not an ordinary mugging, I fancy." As Benson first opened his mouth, then shut it, Forster again tried to nod. "In the pursuit of a good story," said the reporter, "I could always suffer temporary amnesia . . . But I won't." Now the glance was not so much shrewd as conspiratorial. He tried a second time to sit up, with more success now as Benson automatically put out a hand to help him.

"The fearless pursuit of truth in the public interest," said the reporter, "may suit the young, but it doesn't suit an elderly coward like me. Never was much of a one for that sort of caper even when I *was* young. Why I didn't make it on the Street, I suppose . . . Or maybe not. Doesn't matter." A quarter of a century ago it might have mattered to E. M. Forster, but not now.

He looked Benson straight in the eye. "A bargain. Oh, I'll tell you anyway sooner or later—but this could make it sooner, Constable. You help me break out of this Colditz helhole—agree to escort me home so they don't have to waste an ambulance on me. And once I'm safely in my flat with a bottle of Scotch and whatever blasted tablets they give me, I'll tell you what I can remember about the girl who set me up." He frowned. "Slander. Who might have set me up." He corrected himself again. "No, must have done. Because she was after something, I swear—and I only wish I knew what it was."

Nine

THE COATES CHAIN of opticians flourishes nationwide throughout the British Isles except (for reasons not unconnected with the perpetually rain-drenched summer holidays of the founding Coates's childhood) in the Principality of Wales. There are six branches in Allshire alone, including one in the High Street of the county town.

At the end of Saturday's lunchtime rush, the ding-dong of the automatic doorbell hailed one customer coming in as three others hurried out. After a brief sidestepping scuffle on the threshold, the three disappeared while the one stood in the middle of the floor gazing thoughtfully about her.

She was a plump woman in her early thirties, with eyes of a blue so brilliant that she might have been wearing coloured contact lenses. This supposition was borne out by her reply to an assistant's asking if she needed any help.

"Contact lens cleaner, please. Hyaline, if you've got it—a small bottle."

In a Coates shop everything too portable for a manager's peace of mind is kept in a glass case. It took the assistant some moments to unfasten the right door, retrieve the right bottle, rearrange the display, mark on a sheet by the till that the small size of Hyaline was out of stock, and pack the last bottle in a paper bag embossed on both sides with the well-known Coates logo.

An impartial observer might have observed how the plump woman neither tapped her toe nor clicked her tongue with impatience during these proceedings. She seemed happy to go on gazing about the interior of the shop, as if admiring the corporate decorative taste imposed by the Board of Directors—who were based in London—and the local flourishes added by the staff, such as the goldfish mobile over the central desk and the whimsical stickers on the side of the glaucoma pressure-testing machine.

"Anything else, madam?"

"Oh—no, thanks. I think that's the right money."

"Yes, thank you. Exactly right." The till cranked open with an electronic *whirr* as digital figures danced their fluorescent square dance across the black backdrop of the display on the top line. The plump woman nodded, smiled, and slipped her purchase into her handbag. Without another word, she left the shop.

Without another thought, the assistant moved away. What could be less worthy of thought than a purchase of contact lens cleaner?

People were doing it all the time.

PC BENSON SLOWED the panda car to a halt. "We're here," he said. The man in the passenger seat opened his eyes.

"So we are," said E. M. Forster. He glowered in the direction of the sixties block of flats looming over his own, more discreet, Edwardian home. "When we're all dead," he said bitterly, "some developer will buy the freehold and knock the place down and build another concrete monstrosity just like that one." He sighed. "Or worse." He brightened.

"But almost anything's got to be better than that hellhole of a hospital."

"Are you absolutely sure—" began Benson.

"I'm sure," said E. M. Forster. "No booze, no fags, and now I've come out of my trancelike state, no sleep. Those nurses clump up and down the ward giggling and chattering and shushing each other like . . ."

"A herd of elephants?" offered Benson as his passenger fell silent.

The journalist winced at the unoriginality, but said nothing.

With a grunt he lowered his head to focus his gaze on the buckle of his seat belt. His hands scrabbled feebly at his midriff. "Get me out of here," he begged.

It was a slow process to help the invalid out of the car and across to the old red-brick house, though not as slow as Benson might have expected; that Fleet Street training still held. Forster's legs might be a little shaky, but his willpower was not. The thought of the bottle of whisky waiting in his flat spurred him ever onward.

The two men arrived at the front door. "Used to be stained glass in those panels," said Forster. "Survived two world wars—and then they built That Place."

"Even toughened glass breaks," said Benson, "if you hit it hard enough. But," he added sternly with his hand on the round brass knob, "there's no point having toughened glass if you don't bother locking the door. You can't rely on broad daylight nowadays, you know."

"I used to know all the other tenants," said Forster obliquely. "They die off—move away—and now I wouldn't recognise most of the people in this house if they arrived on my doormat with a bottle of Scotch in each hand."

Benson, making a mental note to have a word with the Crime Prevention crowd, opened the door wide and helped the reporter into the hall. He already knew that Forster's flat was up two flights of stairs and there was no lift.

"You're quite sure you can manage, Mr. Forster?" he asked one last time before starting the slow, laborious climb to the second floor.

"Yes," said E. M. Forster through gritted teeth. It was all he said until they finally reached his flat.

Then he said weakly, "Good God."

"Don't touch anything," warned Benson as his companion lurched forward to inspect the damage. "That door's going to need fingerprinting."

"They've smashed the lock," said Forster. "You won't get much off there, will you?"

"We'll do our best, sir. You'd be amazed how stupid some criminals can be, especially the sort of gentry who'd pull a job like this. Stay back now." Benson pushed the invalid gently against the wall and with his elbow shoved the door, which had been pulled shut, open.

After a moment's study, the policeman spoke. "It could be a damn sight worse than it is, believe me, sir. Some of the burglaries I've attended—but you don't want to hear about that."

"I can well imagine." The reporter was at his side, peering in. He essayed a dry chuckle. "I was never one of the tidiest people in the world, but . . ."

"Walk carefully now. Round the edges of the room where they won't have left so many traces—that's right. Can you give me an idea of what's missing?"

E. M. Forster leaned against the table he used as a desk and silently contemplated the ravaged room. Books, where they had not been shoved clumsily to one side to make space, had been tumbled off shelves to the floor. He groaned at the sight of those dog-eared pages, bent covers, and broken spines. The drawers of the small under-table chest he used as a filing cabinet were on the floor with their contents in turmoil. The pile of newspapers he had not yet brought himself to throw away was scattered across the floor. The cardboard boxes in which he kept . . .

"As far as I can tell, nothing," he said at last.

"Er—beg pardon?" But then Benson remembered the concussion. He wished Sergeant Stone were with him. "You've had a shock, sir. And no wonder. Let me take you back to the hospital once I've called in to report this, and—"

"No!" It was a shout, not a calm denial, but Forster did not wince. "I'm perfectly compos mentis, man. Use your brains, can't you? Look! My television's black and white—hardly ever watch the thing—wait until it conks out before I buy another, and then in no hurry to do it. No video recorder. No fancy stereo system, just a steam radio and a gramophone that's seen better days." He stabbed a shaking finger at the desk. "I write everything by hand—no computer, no word processor, typewriter at the office. So . . . nothing worth pinching at all, if we're going to talk about your average crook and his fondness for easy pickings."

"I . . . suppose not," Benson slowly agreed.

"When you're called to a burglary where there's hardly been a thing worth pinching, haven't the buggers usually trashed the place out of sheer spite?"

"Er—quite often, sir," admitted Benson. "But—"

"But they didn't here." E. M. Forster passed a shaking hand over his forehead. Reaction was starting to set in. "Oh, call your print people and your photographers and my insurance company if you like—but this was no ordinary break-in." Heedless of the forensic traces he might be destroying, he dragged out the chair from under the table and sat down. "They had all the time in the world, with my being stuck in hospital." Once more he mopped his brow. "I hate to admit it, but I'm still a sick man. Weak. Couldn't put up much of a show in the way of self-defence. I hope—I just hope they had time enough . . ."

"ME, TOO," TREWLEY said as Benson, fidgeting in his boots, came to the end of his report. "The blighters were looking for something." He rubbed his chin and stared into the distance. "You don't ignore two floors' worth of flats and go straight to the top of a building without knowing in advance that's where you want to be. Your average break-in thug's an idle beggar—won't catch 'em climbing stairs if they haven't got to. This lot did. They knew what they wanted. Wonder if they found it?" Stone stirred on her chair, but said nothing. Trewley grunted. "Well, for poor old Forster's sake I hope they did."

Benson nodded. "He's in no state for he-man tactics if they come back, sir. I, er, thought about asking one of the neighbours to be a—a sort of bodyguard until he's had the lock fixed, but he says he doesn't know any of 'em. Which isn't surprising, sir, with such a big old house."

"Nice thick walls," interposed Trewley. "No wonder they never heard a thing."

"No, sir. I mean, yes." Benson's fingers twitched along the seams of his trousers as he stood to attention with his arms at his sides. "And I, er, wasn't sure we could spare a man to stay with him . . ."

"We can't," said Trewley. "More's the pity, because if they didn't find it, whatever it is—yes, Sergeant?"

"It might have been a warning, sir," said Stone. "Not actually looking for anything, perhaps. Just telling Forster to—oh, to keep quiet about what he knows about the bank business, for example. I mean—we did wonder, even before this happened, didn't we?"

"Coincidence. Umph." The superintendent glared at Benson. "Stop wriggling like that, for heaven's sake. If you've got something to say, then say it."

"Sir," said Benson, ramrod-stiff. "He said the girl—woman," he amended with a wary eye on Sergeant Stone, "was pumping him about the robbery most of the evening, sir, but he didn't say a dickybird. He, er, says," he added. "But maybe when she told him he wasn't spilling any beans, that's when they decided to do the place over to—to find . . . whatever it was they wanted, sir."

"Or," Trewley mused, "to remind him to keep quiet, as the sergeant here suggested. Could be." He started tapping with his paperknife on the blotter. "This female inquisitor—would he know her again?"

"He says yes, sir. But—well, you know how it is. Can be, I mean. With . . . everything . . ."

"If she has any sense," said Stone after a moment or two of silence, "she'll be miles away by now. What about the chap who introduced them?"

"He says peas in a pod, Sarge—Sergeant," amended the wretched Benson. "You—you know Mr. Forster likes his drink." Stone, and Trewley, nodded. Benson braced himself. "Well, reading between the lines, this chap made out he knew him and Forster went along with it to save his face, but really he wouldn't be able to take his oath *who* it was. Except that he had a leather jacket with studs, which only means half the tearaways in Allingham instead of the whole gaggle of 'em. Sir," said Benson hurriedly as the superintendent muttered.

"Is it any use bringing him in to look at mug shots?" Stone asked, to spare her superior's feelings.

Benson sighed. "Not today, he says, and I can't say I

blame him, Sarge—*ant*," he added. Trewley snorted. Stone gave the hapless young man an encouraging smile. Benson took heart. "He looks like death warmed up, and if I'd been the hospital I'd've kept him in—but he would insist. And he did look better for the Scotch, Sarge, though I wasn't too happy about it at first. And I promised to go round tomorrow morning on the off chance he'll feel well enough to come in about lunchtime to look at a few pictures. And if he isn't tomorrow, then he says he'll do his best Monday, if that's what we want."

"Sir?" Stone turned to Trewley, who was muttering again. "What do you think?"

"I think," he said after a ponderous pause, "that this blue-eyed tottie of Forster's would be our best bet." On her chair, Detective Sergeant Stone moved restlessly. The superintendent glanced at her, but she remained silent. He made a mental note that she would pitch into him once Benson had gone, and soldiered apologetically on.

"This, uh, woman," he said, with another sideways look at his sergeant: Who still said nothing, but said it with somewhat less severity. "If we could lay our hands on her, she's the one who can tell us what the hell's going on—except that you're probably right, Stone. She'll be miles away by now. A pity. It was clever. She was, what, ten years older than the bloke in studs?" From the corner of his eye he saw his sergeant give the idea serious consideration. "A woman of the world," he continued with relish, rolling lugubrious eyes in Benson's direction. The young constable blushed.

A rumbling chuckle came from the bulldog's throat. "Flattering to have her pick him out from the crowd the way she did, according to Forster. Very clever. Nice and safe and anonymous for her, and it made him feel important. He'll have talked big, of course, the way these young men do. Eh, Benson?"

Benson blushed still more. Stone said quickly, "And he'll have been all the more annoyed when she dropped him after making the acquaintance of Forster. Once he'd outlived his usefulness." Her eyes were bright as the possible convolutions began to present themselves. "Just suppose . . . we're wrong that this was all to do with the bank robbery. Suppose she really did want to know what it's like to be a reporter taking eyewitness statements and being on the spot in the middle of the action—"

"Forster?" exclaimed Trewley. "He's the laziest beggar in the county. How he's kept his job all this time—talk about walking a tightrope—he hasn't covered a big story in years, and the only reason he got this one was because he happened to be hanging around the market watching the video blighters."

"Yes, sir," said Stone with great patience. "That's my point. Forster manages to survive in a—an increasingly competitive world. Maybe Blue-Eyes was genuinely impressed. Wanted to know how he did—does—it. She wangles an introduction through our friend in the studs who talks himself up to her as the one who knows what's what—and who's who—and then he finds himself ignored." She allowed her glance to fall first on Trewley, then on Benson. "Men can be very touchy about these things. Suppose Mr. Studs was the one who lay in wait for Forster and attacked him on his way home from the pub out of jealousy?"

There was a pregnant pause. Benson looked firmly at his boots. Stone looked innocently at the ceiling.

"Forster's got to come in on Monday at the latest," decreed Trewley at last. "Not that I necessarily agree with you, Sergeant. I don't like coincidence, which is what it would be according to you. One bloke working on his own has a go at Forster, while another bloke decides to do his flat—talk about too much of a good thing."

"They could have been working together," offered Stone. "Or Studs could have done one after the other. For some reason entirely unconnected with the bank robbery or—or anything else we know about now."

"Umph." Trewley's imagination was starting to boggle. "Yes. Well . . . When Forster's feeling better, we want a detailed statement from him . . . But let's go with what we have for now. Why Miss Blue-Eyes in the pub? No matter what sort of coincidence she is or isn't. If Chummie was planning to bash *or* burgle Forster later—for whatever reason—why should he risk bringing himself to Forster's attention that way? I know villains are stupid, but as stupid as that? He would've done far better to palm her off on someone else for the introduction—Yes, Benson?"

Benson coughed. He glanced at Stone, who winked. With a sigh, he spoke. "He . . . might have wanted to take the opportunity to make sure he'd got the right bloke before he did him, sir. And the blue-eyed bint—sorry, Sarge!" The look on Stone's face was not friendly. "The, er, blue-eyed woman," said Benson apologetically, "was a better excuse than anything he could come up with on his own. Sir. Sergeant. Er."

Trewley and Stone exchanged glances. Trewley said after a moment, "All right, push off. When Forster comes in for his game of I-Spy, let me know . . . So, now," he said as the door closed behind the unfortunate young constable. "Coincidence, stupidity, or something more?"

"Something more," Stone decided after only a brief hesitation. "I think," prudence made her add. "Probably."

Trewley grinned. "We could speculate for hours, but it won't get us anywhere. Dabs and Snaps'll come back to us when they can—if they can . . ." The superintendent, while having the highest opinion of his fingerprint and photographic scenes-of-crime departments, would never tempt fate by hoping out loud for good news. "But until they do," he went on glumly, "we're on our own. Like Forster."

He cocked a quizzical eyebrow at his sergeant. "A panda or two might make their presence, um, obvious over the next couple of days," she suggested.

"But?" he prompted as she paused.

"But Forster's not the only one to worry about, is he, sir? If the woman—by herself or with fifty, um, accomplices—*was* interested in the bank robbery, there were other eyewitnesses." She frowned. "Unless, of course, there was something in particular Forster saw that nobody else did."

"Him and everyone else in the market square," Trewley reminded her. She sighed and said nothing.

He rubbed his chin as he made up his mind. "We'd better play it safe. The Allshire and National business could well be tied up with what happened to Forster, though we haven't a clue how. And it could be something else entirely, though we'll assume for the moment it's not. So, there's always a chance that the others who witnessed the raid could be running the same risks as him. We've got a list of names and addresses. We'll have the panda lot check 'em all out very visibly for the next few days—and hope that's enough," he added gravely. "But the sooner we get Forster in here to look at mug shots, the better. Studs is the first anything-like-decent lead we've got in the bank business so far. If he *is* involved, we want to find him. Apart from anything else, we want to discourage him and his pals from any more of the same little tricks they've pulled already."

He looked thoughtfully at his sergeant. "You're the one with the medical training. What are our chances of getting any sense out of the man tomorrow, rather than on Monday?"

She sighed in response to the question he had not asked. "All right. I'll pop round later this afternoon. I'll tell him it's a follow-up visit to check on Forensic—and I only hope they don't find out, or my name will be mud."

Trewley grinned. "You can cope with Forensic, Stone. I have every faith in you. If there's a snowball's chance in hell you can get Forster here tomorrow, you'll do it."

Detective Sergeant Stone did not reply.

Ten

THE SIGN OVER the window was lettered in peeling black on age-discoloured white: GADGETT & SON: GENERAL HANDYMAN AND SUPPLIES. It looked as if it hadn't been painted since the line beneath had been inscribed. *Est. 1927.* The breathless man in the anonymous blue anorak felt his heart beat faster as he pushed open the door.

Bert Gadgett, a bright little button of a character in late middle age, looked up and then blinked at the jangling of the bell. "Ah," he said, neatly folding the newspaper in which he had been engrossed and dropping it on the counter. "Afternoon, sir—and you're in luck, that you are. Another five minutes and I'd have been putting up the shutters."

The newcomer, breathing more slowly, forced himself to speak without hurry or embarrassment. There was no sense in letting the shopkeeper know that this was his last port of call. That everywhere else in Allingham had been unable to help him.

If Gadgett's couldn't help him . . .

He could only ask. "Locks," he said, trying not to gasp or splutter. "Window locks. Security."

Bert was nodding energetically. Was this a hopeful sign? "H-have you," enquired the man in the dark blue anorak, "anything suitable in stock?"

Bert stopped nodding and grinned at him. "Well now, not so much as we had a few days ago, sir. They're on order, of course, but since market day—but there, we've still enough for your needs, I reckon." There came a sign of relief from the worried man. Bert nodded again. "For a house this would be, would it?"

"Yes," said the man in the dark blue anorak.

"Ah," said Bert. "What sort of windows?"

"W-what? I mean—well—glass, of course."

"No," said Bert, humouring the poor ignoramus whose face was so pale and worried. "Wood, metal, or plastic frames?" he asked. "Sash or casement? Double glazing? Most of them's got special integral locks, see. So that's the sort of thing I need to know. See?"

"Oh," breathed the man in the dark blue anorak with a shudder. "How stupid of me. Yes. Uh—they're the original wooden frames. And the sort of window that opens, uh, sideways."

Bert translated this to himself, gazed at the man with the pale face, fished out his receipt pad from under the counter, tore off and turned over the top sheet, and drew on the back. "Like this?"

"Yes." Gasp. "Yes—can you help me?"

"How many windows?"

"T-ten."

Bert recognised the need for caution. "Sorry, sir, what I meant to say was how many struts? Some of your windows'll open double, I don't doubt."

"Uh-oh. Yes." The man rubbed a hand over his face. "Yes, I wrote it down somewhere . . ."

After much frantic delving into pockets, the piece of paper on which he had noted measurements and other details was unearthed. In all the frenzy of visiting the earlier establishments it had become buried and almost forgotten. Bert Gadgett took it, studied it, and pursed his lips, which made the man in the anorak shudder again. Then, slowly, Bert said, "I'll have to check out the back, but I reckon there's enough left for the ground floor, at any rate."

"I'll take anything you've got," said the man in the dark blue anorak urgently.

And he did.

• • •

THE HANDS OF the office clock were almost together for noon.

"Roll on Monday, that's what I say." Superintendent Trewley stretched himself and yawned. His chair creaked and rocked on its castors. "A pity you couldn't persuade Forster to drop by this morning . . . but you did your best, I've no doubt."

"It didn't take a medical expert to see he was in no fit state to start peering at dozens of mug shots even twenty-four hours later," said Stone firmly. "And I think Monday might be pushing our luck." She forced a smile. "After all, sir, we wouldn't want him dying from delayed shock in an interview room, would we? You know disposing of the body is always the most difficult part."

"Not necessarily." The superintendent, as weary as his sergeant of checking and re-checking a mass of reports that were apparently leading nowhere, was of a mind to be argumentative. "I'd have said finding a foolproof method of murder was the most difficult. Untraceable poisons. That sort of thing."

"You can't beat the good old-fashioned gloves and blunt instrument," said Stone rather wistfully. She had come in on her day off two days running, but by now she was heartily wishing she hadn't bothered.

"Buy you a drink?" offered Trewley as he observed her wilt. "We've slaved over this blasted bumf quite long enough for now. Talk about dead ends and no blasted leads. A change of scene will do us good. Or do you need to get home to cook Young What's-His-Name his dinner?"

"He's every bit as capable of opening a tin as I am," Stone said sternly. Teasing was all very well, but there were limits. "Or of shoving something in the microwave." She smiled again, more easily this time. "Yes, thanks. A drink sounds fine."

To avoid barbed remarks from the eagle-eyed Desk Sergeant Pleate about dereliction of duty, they sneaked out through the back door of the police station, hardly daring to draw breath until they were safely ensconced in the saloon bar of The Spice Trader. It took time to find a table, but in the end Stone sat down to enjoy a tomato juice with a Worcestershire dash, while Trewley savoured a pint of Old Guvnor and dipped absently into his sergeant's packet of crisps as soon as he'd finished his own.

"My round," said Stone, as the last cheese-and-onion crumb was shaken briskly into her superior's hand. "I can take a hint. Same again, sir? Or would you prefer me to have smoky bacon this time?"

He had the grace to grin an apology as she collected the empties and vanished into the crowd. She was a good girl. One of the best. Knew when to nag him about his diet and when to leave him in peace. "Smoky bacon," he murmured in happy anticipation, then chuckled as he recalled how she had once wreaked tacit revenge for his crisp-napping habit by buying one of the new varieties and letting him eat half the packet before drawing his attention to the flavour. Artificial, she'd explained as he spluttered. Nevertheless . . .

"Hedgehog," he rumbled. "Hedgehog!"

"And hello to you, Mr. Trewley. Wasn't sure you'd seen me. Busy, ain't it?"

The superintendent had jumped when first addressed, but soon recognised the bright button eyes and chirpy voice of Bert Gadgett. Hedgehog. Above all the chatter it was an easy mistake, he supposed. "Hello, Mr. Gadgett. Quite a scrum in here today. How are things?"

"Oh, mustn't grumble—or maybe I should." The little man winked. "Another week like the one just gone, and we'll be taking our next holiday abroad. You can't beat England, that's what I say, but the wife's keen, and I've only kept her here by saying we can't afford it." He tapped a finger to the side of his nose and winked again. "She does the day-to-day books, see, but the fancy figuring's my side of the business."

"And business is booming," deduced Trewley, who could guess why and saw it almost as a personal affront. "Locks and bolts and burglar alarms, eh?"

Bert nodded. "You'll be having your work cut to find them," he said sagely. "Gone to ground, that's what they'll have done if they've any sense, not that these young thugs has got much sense or they'd know your lot'll get 'em in the end. You in here watching for blokes what spends more money than they did rightly ought to have?"

"Could be," said Trewley. And Bert winked again.

"Her comes your young lady assistant." Mr. Gadgett put out a helping hand for the tray. "Need any help with that, miss? Haven't seen you for a while. Keeping well?"

"Thanks, Mr. Gadgett." Stone flashed him a smile as she allowed him to relieve her of her burden. "As well as can be expected," she said cheerfully.

"Ah, that's what I was saying to your boss here. You'll find those shotgun devils sooner or later, mark my words. Bit of excitement, though, eh? Allingham on the telly!"

"Some of us," rumbled Trewley, "would prefer a little less excitement, Mr. Gadgett."

"Myself, I ain't one of your nervous types," said Bert, who most definitely was not. "The wife, now . . ."

Trewley and Stone remembered Mrs. Bert as being the complement to end all spousal complements. Like her husband, she was bright and chirpy, but when he was speaking, she was silent; and when she was in full flow, he never said a word. They seemed to live their lives in a perfect vocal equilibrium, since neither ever disagreed with what the other had to say. It was hard to envisage their emotional life as being other than equally well-balanced.

Trewley spotted the logo on his new packet of crisps. It showed a small, pointy-nosed creature covered in spikes. "The ladies," he said at once without looking at Stone, "are bound to be more sensitive, Mr. Gadgett. The weaker sex, with all due respect to my sergeant here." Stone was heard to mutter something not in the least respectful, though Trewley spoke with all the authority of a man with a wife and three daughters.

"The men, too, Mr. Trewley," said Bert before Stone could mutter again. "Not wishing to contradict you," he went on, "but there's been as many gents as ladies come in after locks and bolts these past few days—like yesterday, now. Well, if you say it's the ladies who worry most I'd have to disagree mightily, sir. Mightily! I tell you, just before closing time he comes in, green as grass and a-puffing and blowing in his haste, and have I got any locks for windows and doors, and he'll take the lot *and* a drill for fitting 'em himself rather than pay me to call round later and do it for him. Which is to say next morning, with it being almost dark by then—though I'd've gladly done it and not charged double for Sunday, seeing who the poor bloke was and understanding well why he should be in such a state."

"Oh. Why?" asked Stone, making polite conversation as Trewley, still annoyed about the hedgehog crisps, frowned at her. He'd come to the pub to relax, not to have a blow-by-blow account of a handyman's daily life recounted in tedious detail. Except . . .

"Yes," he said, before Bert could reply. Stone might just be on to something here, after all. "Who was this nervous gentleman? And why should he be so upset?"

"Ah, now." Bert scratched his head. "That I can't tell you, in a manner of speaking—and then to put it another way I can, seeing as how I don't know who he was, but I know *who* he was, if you get my meaning."

"I'm afraid we don't, Mr. Gadgett," said Stone above the exasperated snorts of her superior. Bert, luckily, was so busy enjoying being the centre of attention that he noticed nothing. He grinned at his bewildered audience and winked.

"What was I saying earlier about the telly? And that's who he was, poor bloke, with his head all bandaged then as was only a plaster yesterday, though still walking a bit shaky, for which I can't say I blame him. Been in hospital, he told me. Concussion. And if he gets to worrying that those shotgun devils might know where he lives and how he could identify them, well, small wonder to me that he wanted a few locks and bolts on his windows and doors, because sure as eggs if it'd been me I'd've wanted the same."

"Ah," said Trewley. He looked at Stone. "Not an eyewitness from *outside* the bank, then." Through gritted teeth he now addressed Bert. "So you recognised him from the television pictures, Mr. Gadgett?"

"I did indeed, Mr. Trewley. Knew him at once though, not

wishing to presume, I said nothing to him until he'd decided what he wanted and paid for it. Just passed the time of day, see, while I was doing the parcel."

"As I recall," Stone said slowly, "there were several people filmed coming down the bank steps. Do you happen to know who he was, Mr. Gadgett?"

Bert tapped the side of his nose once more. "Indeed I do, miss, and if that don't show you it pays to stay within the law, then I don't know what does. There's many a self-employed man, naming no names, would knock something off for cash and not charge the tax."

Trewley muttered something about the black economy, and Stone nodded for Bert to continue, which he did. "But me," he said, "I like my paperwork honest, I do. And if it's more than a few pounds they're paying, I'll take a cheque, on account of how too much cash in the till or in the pocket is asking for trouble from them that aren't as honest as me." He shook his head. "Putting temptation in their way, see?"

"So you don't put it," said Stone, as her superior muttered again. "I call that very sensible and public-spirited of you, Mr. Gadgett."

"Very," snapped Trewley. "But *who was it?*"

"Name of Ross," said Bert, startled out of his leisurely narrative flow by the vehemence of the superintendent's tone. "Printed on his cheque, see, and the signature matched the card all right, so I knew it weren't stolen . . ."

It took the two detectives a while to disentangle themselves from the handyman once they were confident he had nothing more to tell them. They won their liberty in the end when Stone chose to muse aloud on the dietary merits of crisps and nothing else for a Sunday lunch. Bert remembered the roast and two vegetables waiting for him at home and hurried off.

"What do you make of that, sir?" Stone jiggled the dregs of her tomato juice around the bottom of her glass.

"Umph." Trewley gave the empty crisp packets a hungry look. "Could be he's just the nervous type. You know the way some people who've had burglars end up moving house because they can't stand the thought that someone's been poking around their personal territory."

"Understandable," murmured Stone, still jiggling. She sat up. "Nobody in the market square came close enough to the robbery to recognise anyone, did they?"

"If they did, they haven't said so to us." Trewley was feeling hungrier by the minute. At such times he was always inclined to pessimism. "Could be someone did, of course. And they're keeping quiet because they want a slice of the action, silly fools. Blackmail."

"Seriously, sir, can you see Forster as a blackmailer?"

Trewley sighed. "I'd like to know why he was attacked and his flat done over," he said. "*And* I'd like to know whether or not it's for fear of the same that friend Ross has got the wind up. None of the pandas reported anybody else with their knickers in a twist last night."

"But they didn't report Ross either," Stone wanted to remind him.

The objection was ignored. "I don't like coincidence," he said, though he had no real need to tell her this. "Forster and Ross, both scared. Both living alone with nobody to raise the alarm, not until it might be too late. Both witnesses to the robbery—but in different places, dammit. Forster. Ross. What's the link between them?"

Stone jumped to her feet. "Coincidence," she said with a perfectly straight face. "My round," she added as the bulldog opened his mouth to roar. "A pie and a pint?"

She had to queue, which made Trewley's hungry impatience all the greater, but within half an hour he was another man. "I needed that," he said, setting knife and fork together on the plate and leaning back on his chair to ease his trouser waistband. Stone prudently said nothing.

The superintendent stretched himself and prepared for action. "If you've finished digesting, come on."

"Come where?" was his sergeant's pertinent response as she hurried after him to the car parked outside.

"To visit Paul Ross," Trewley told her. "As the routine work is being done by everyone else—or if it isn't I'll have their guts for garters when I find out—it's time for a spot of detective work. We want . . ." He shrugged. "Inspiration. Visit the scene of the crime and see what happens. And don't," he warned as she was about to speak, "tell me it's not a crime for a bloke to buy a spot of home security. I know. What I don't know, in this case, is *why* he bought it."

"You can hardly come right out with it and ask him, can you, sir?" Bulldog he might be, but bullheaded he was not. Usually. "The poor chap will think he's living in a police state and we're checking up on his every move. Heaven help him if he's gone and bought sugarcoated cornflakes instead of the sort with extra fibre."

"Oh, we're checking up on him all right. You're medically trained, aren't you? So we're paying a nice friendly follow-up call now he's had a few days out of hospital." He grinned. "Or if you prefer, it's a nice friendly routine crime-prevention call. He won't wonder at that if he spotted any of the pandas prowling around in the dark." And the superintendent favoured their own anonymous, unmarked police car with an ambiguous stare.

"I'd prefer the crime-prevention story, thanks." Stone was unlocking the driver's door as she spoke. "He might ask me to look at his bandage, and—well, sir, I'd prefer not to have to. No matter how honourable the intention."

Trewley felt privately that anyone still bleeding after three days shouldn't have been discharged from hospital in the first place, but he said nothing out loud. "Crime prevention it is," he agreed, glancing at his watch. "With luck he'll be washing his pots and pans after dinner, and won't have time to start his afternoon nap . . ."

But when they arrived at the address it was to find Paul Ross not at home. "Eats fast," was Trewley's only comment.

"Or he's sleeping it off," said Stone. "With earplugs, so he can't hear anyone at the door. Doors." They had tried both, with no success at either.

Trewley rubbed his chin. "Back to the station, then. We've skived off long enough." Stone said nothing. Trewley sighed. "*I* have," he said in deference to her interrupted day off. "And for all our grand talk of inspiration, we haven't really come up with any—"

"Oi!" came a bellow from behind them. Only the years of exposure to Trewley's bulldog roar stopped Stone clapping her hands to her startled ears.

Both detectives turned to see a very large man with a very red face standing beside a rotary mower in the middle of the lawn of the house next door. "Oi!" he cried again, as they walked towards him back down Paul Ross's front path. "You the Old Bill?"

"We are police officers," Trewley confirmed as soon as he was within comfortable distance of the red-faced man.

The man rolled his eyes. "Too late, arncher! Where were you this morning? I tell you, they're never arahnd when you need 'em, that's the trouble."

Trewley's tone sharpened. "There was some trouble at this address earlier today?" The closed, locked, silent home of the bank robbery hostage . . .

"Bleeding near murder," said the red-faced man. Trewley and Stone stood still. "And me," went on Red Face, "what's always been a law-abiding man more than happy to be the murderer, I tell you—and not the only one, neither. Why, I could name you a dozen folk living not a million miles from Mr. Bleeding Pandemonium Ross who'd have done him in and not have their conscience trouble 'em in the least."

"Umph," said Trewley. "We take it that you managed to restrain yourselves."

Red Face leaned massive elbows on the mower handle. "It was a close thing, I tell you. Soon as it were light he was making as much racket over there as a whole bleeding site full of builders. Electric drills, hammering—you never heard such an uproar in your life. And," he added bitterly, "on a Sunday, too, when a man likes a bit of a lie-in after having to get up early all week. We tried telling him, but would he bleeding listen?"

"Probably not," Trewley said.

"I'm telling you," said the red-faced man. "All right for him, weren't it? He knew to expect what he was doing. But talk about unexpected for the rest of us poor devils. Fair turned you over, all that bleeding noise and upset so early in the morning."

"It must have been dreadful," sympathised Stone as the superintendent, busy thinking, said nothing. "Did it go on for long?"

"Long enough." Red Face stared through narrowed eyes at the vacant windows of the house next door. "Can't blame him for pushing off like he did the minute he was done drilling. He knew there'd be more words said by folk as didn't care for being seen in their pyjamas coming round once they was decent to give him a piece of their mind. Back under cover of dark, too, I shouldn't wonder. Hoping we'll have forgotten—which we won't in a hurry, I tell you." He shook his head sadly. "Bleeding fool. If he'd only waited a couple of hours, who would've minded? Not me, for one. Live and let live, that's what I say. There's plenty of blokes does their own repairs and suchlike to save paying someone else. But him—he's never done such a thing in three bleeding years. And then he suddenly goes and wakes everyone for miles the minute the sun comes up. Can't think what's got into him. Must be that bump on the head the other day's turned him demented . . ."

But Trewley and Stone suspected there might be rather more to it than that.

Eleven

A ONE-WOMAN BUSINESS cannot afford to have its staff take time off except for the most pressing of reasons. Challenge must be met with ingenuity. A sprained wrist encouraged Karen Crabtree to leave for work well before her usual hour on Monday morning, knowing that she must be less than prompt in her dealings for the rest of the day—if not the week—until the swelling went down.

There were few signs of life in any of the nearby shops as she approached the Eye Deal door. The newsagent gave her a cheerily sympathetic greeting when she popped in to buy a packet of chocolate biscuits and a paper, but the grocer's blinds remained down, as did the shutters of her immediate neighbour, the off-licence. A post-office van about to pull away from the just-emptied pillarbox paused for the driver to see whether she carried any letters before rattling off in a cloud of diesel fumes.

Karen coughed, fumbled in her bag, produced her key, and applied it to the lock. She had to twist the key in just the right way before the door would open, and with her swollen wrist it took several goes before she managed it. She opened the door, and the pottery bells clattered overhead. She bent to pick up a small pile of post from the mat, and as she closed the door, the bells clattered again.

She carried the letters over to the desk and put her bag inside the bottom drawer, which she locked, though clumsily. She was even more clumsy as she tried to clip the key on the plaster ring in her pocket, but this, too, she managed in the end. A one-woman business cannot afford to be sloppy in matters of security.

She stood quite still, listening. The bells had long since stopped clattering. The door was shut.

She did not move. She listened. She cocked her head to one side and listened again. She hadn't noticed earlier—she had been too preoccupied—but . . . something was wrong. Wasn't it?

"Too much noise," the optician told herself at last. "Unless," she added—a scientific training prepares one to see at least both sides of any question—"I'm all het up and oversensitive because of my wretched wrist. Yes, that must be it. Delayed shock, of course."

It wasn't until she was struggling to put a cardboard box of rubbish outside the back door that she realised her scientific training had, for once, let her down.

TREWLEY AND STONE had also gone early to work. Just after nine the superintendent began muttering to himself. Without a word, Stone slipped from her seat and left the room.

She came back from the police canteen with two mugs of tea, a plate of sticky buns, and a snippet of advance information from PC Benson that would help the superintendent score a Brownie point or two when he studied the daily occurrence report compiled by Desk Sergeant Pleate and, in the nature of things, presented for Trewley's attention some hours after the events recorded had taken place.

As Stone and her laden tray appeared around the office door, Trewley threw his morning paper to one side and tried to look as if he had been working nonstop since she left. His sergeant discreetly said nothing as she handed him his share of the late-breakfast goodies, but dropped into the visitors' chair and settled herself for a short spell of professional gossip.

"There's been an attempted break-in at that little optician's on the new estate," she said. "Eye Deal. That's not where you go, is it, sir?"

Trewley grunted a denial as he picked up his mug. He still

disliked having to acknowledge his need for reading glasses. "Attempted," he echoed. "They didn't get in?"

"A broken window, that's all. It looks as if they must have been interrupted—the back alley is a short cut from the pub, remember."

"Lovers' Lane, more like." Trewley thought of his three nubile daughters and shuddered at what the future might hold. "Though why anyone should want to do their courting down there is anyone's guess."

Stone could guess what he was thinking. "It's anyone's guess what a burglar would want from an optician's," she said hurriedly. "Benson thinks they made a mistake and were really trying to break into the off-licence next door, but I'm not so sure. Even if they were interrupted they could have come back later and tried again, but he checked with the off-licence people, and they say they didn't."

"Probably back tonight, then." Trewley frowned at the calendar on the wall. Five years ago, when he could still think of himself as in his prime, he wouldn't have been able to read it. Now, as age and long sight crept up on him, he could. "Or next weekend," he added. "Give 'em longer before anyone notices. If," he said witheringly, "any of the villains around here are capable of planning that far ahead."

"Or with such logic," supplied Stone absently. She, too, was frowning, though for a different reason. "There's nothing in an optician's that's worth pinching, as far as I know. It isn't as if a druggie could get a buzz from, oh, contact lens cleaner, or the stuff they use to impregnate polishing cloths . . ."

Trewley, with his daughters in mind, winced at her careless choice of verb; but his interest had been caught. "You never know with villains," he said, picking up the paper he had been so quick to discard. "It says here there's a gang of shoplifters in Warwickshire who only pinch toothpaste, for heaven's sake. Sixty tubes they got away with from the latest place—and don't try telling me they're worried about their children's teeth, because I won't believe you."

"A minor brush with the law," offered Stone with a grin. "Sorry, sir."

"So you should be." The bloodhound eyes were twinkling now. Her nonsense always cheered him up. "But that's the seventh time, according to this. Toothpaste! They must be out of their tiny minds."

"Then perhaps it's not so far-fetched an idea that some-one might be unhinged enough to want to rob an optician's. Should we put out a general alert to keep an eye open for shortsighted loonies? I wonder—"

The telephone rang. Trewley was busy with his sticky bun. Stone knew what to do.

"Mr. Trewley's office," she told the telephone. "What?" she cried ten seconds later. "Yes—look—wait just a minute . . ." She clapped her hand over the mouthpiece and addressed her superior. "I know you don't like coinci-dence, sir, but Sergeant Pleate reports a break-in at the local branch of Hobson's Choice. The optician's," she added as he stared at her.

He swallowed the rest of his bun in one mighty gulp. "I know what they are. That's where I got mine. A successful attempt this time, I gather."

"They got in through the back, the same way they tried at Eye Deal," said Stone. "And it seems they were disturbed this time as well, sir. There are signs of a struggle—and the man who lives in the flat upstairs is missing."

Trewley stared at her again. "Kidnapped?" he enquired as she waited for instructions. "Who was he?"

The telephone quacked in his sergeant's hand. When the superintendent wanted to know something, his voice was not always muted.

Stone listened. "It's Mr. Paine," she reported. Trewley leaned over the desk to snatch the telephone from her.

"Pleate," he barked, "is that Paine the optician who's disappeared?" Stone could not hear the sergeant's reply, but from the look on the superintendent's face she could guess the answer. "We're on our way," Trewley said and banged the handset on its cradle so hard that the pens in his marmalade jar rocked to and fro.

He jumped to his feet. "Come on," he said, striding from the room with Stone close behind him. "You're right," he told her. "I don't like coincidence, and this is coincidence with knobs on—and I don't mean because Paine's the bloke who did my eye test for me. In today's paper," he said over his shoulder as he stumped around a corner of the corridor. "And I don't mean the toothpaste, Stone. There's an optician missing from somewhere up north—Leeds, I think—and they suspect that she's been kidnapped."

AT HOBSON'S CHOICE the plump matron, pale but determined, was on the telephone trying her best to persuade a peevish client that his mid-morning appointment had indeed, and for reasons beyond anyone's control, been cancelled at the last minute. The young man with the charming smile was not smiling now. He sat on one of the low armchairs, his blank eyes shifting, over and over again, between the Closed sign on the shop door and the clock on the wall above the middle of the three anti-tilt filing cabinets.

"I can't believe it," he kept saying. "Not Mr. Paine!"

"You drink your tea, sir. You'll feel better with something inside you." PC Benson wished Sergeant Stone would come. "Drink up," he begged. "Mrs. Milner," he called gently as the plump matron decided to let the wretched man have a wasted journey and hung up on him, "do come and tell Mr. Waghorn he's doing himself no good behaving this way. Or Mr. Paine," he added. "When the super gets here, he'll want to know every little detail if he's going to be able to help."

"The constable is right, Richard." Mrs. Milner, shock or no shock, belonged to a generation that prided itself on having more mental fortitude than the unhappy Waghorn. "Do try to pull yourself together," she said, though not unkindly. She picked up his neglected cup of tea with hands that hardly trembled and held it out to him. "Drink some of this. Drooping about the place keening in that ridiculous manner is helping nobody."

A brisk rapping made them all—even young Waghorn—

look round. The unmistakable face of Superintendent Trewley surveyed them through the door, with Sergeant Stone just visible at his side and two blurred, masculine shapes behind him. Benson hurried to let his colleagues in.

First he showed them the broken window at the rear of the shop, the glass fragments on the floor sticky with honey, and torn pieces of paper. "An old-fashioned idea," muttered Trewley, "but it usually works. More's the pity."

"We'll dust for prints," said one of the masculine shapes who carried a black leather bag.

"We'll check for fibres," said the other shape, fingering the expensive camera slung around his neck. "And a few photos wouldn't hurt, either."

"Smashed the window to get in," Trewley said as he surveyed the evidence. "And used the door to get out. Easier than climbing, especially if you've got someone with you who doesn't want to come. You carry on down here," he told the two from Forensic. "Sergeant Stone and I will see what Benson has to show us."

"Now that's clever," said Stone, once they were back in the main body of the shop. "I would hardly have known that door was there if you hadn't pointed it out."

"Pretty good camouflage," agreed Benson. Stone smothered the words *trompe l'oeil* and simply nodded. "Hidden by that funny bit of wall the way it is, too," he added. "Some sort of eye test, maybe, this being an optician's and all."

"Gets round the planning bylaws nicely," said Trewley the cynic. "Very clever. They wanted to expand the business but they didn't want to have to go to the trouble of finding new premises. So they thought about going sideways, only the stairs up from the road to the flat were in their way. You can see how they knocked down the dividing wall and built that one out and round, and then blocked up the door to the road and made the sole means of access through the shop."

"Which means the burglars might not have known there was anyone living above the shop when they broke in," interposed Stone. "As the original, um, visible outside door has been . . . well, lost."

Trewley, rubbing his chin, contemplated the camouflaged internal door in silence for a moment or two. "They might not be local, you mean? Yes." He frowned. "*I* knew because I've been in here before—and anyway I remember the mess while the builders were doing the job. But how about local people who don't have their eyes tested here?"

Stone gave him a sideways look. "I imagine very few locals are unaware of what went on, sir," she said, rather drily. The traffic chaos caused by the accidental marketday dropping of a builders' skip to block both lanes of the road at once was etched in her memory as yet another of her partner's traffic-generated nightmares.

Benson stifled a chuckle. Trewley grunted. She could be right; and even if she wasn't, it was a theory worth bearing in mind . . . Yet it was hardly conclusive proof that the break-in had been committed by burglars (if not kidnappers) from out of town. They really knew little more than when they had first arrived.

And they hadn't been the first to arrive. "You know," said Trewley as Benson, catching his eye, stopped grinning and moved to open the camouflaged door with the tip of a wary boot, "I've always felt sorry for poor old Paine. He can't be far off retirement. Suppose they don't let him stay in the flat once he's not working for them any longer? Doubt if they'll make it one of the perks—or if they do, they'll take it off his pension, I dare say."

But then his voice became more grave than complaining as he added, "Assuming he lives long enough to draw it, that is. Bloke his age dragged out of his home after a struggle and taken who knows where . . ."

"The evidence would suggest a roughhouse of some sort, sir," agreed Stone cautiously as she followed his gaze. The door had creaked open to give a clear view of the lower part of the stairs, complete with scuff marks on the drugget and hints of one or two darker, more sinister marks that might bear closer investigation. Or, in Stone's case, might not. From the top landing a pale yellow rhomboid of electric light illuminated one side of the stairway to show pictures hanging crookedly on the wall nearest the door to the main body of the shop. "Mr. Paine," said Stone slowly, "is a tidy-minded man as I recall. I don't think he would leave the place looking like this in the normal run of things."

"Benson," said Trewley. "Did either of those two go up to the flat before they reported the break-in?"

"Switch the lights on, you mean, sir?" Benson coughed. "Mrs. Milner is willing to swear she never touched a thing." He caught Stone's look of surprise. "Well, she didn't need to, with it being daytime—and, uh, Mr. Waghorn didn't go upstairs at all, Sarge. Sir," he added unhappily, embarrassed for the frailty of his fellow man.

"Light left on all night, then," said Trewley.

"And his door left open, too," said Stone. "It certainly looks as if he heard something and came downstairs to find out what was going on—"

"Unless," broke in Trewley, "he faked the whole thing. Easy enough to do. Though I can't see why he should," he added. He scowled. "Probably find he's been helping himself to the takings for years. It's always the quiet ones you've got to watch—and yes, Sergeant, I do know that's slander. We'll check upstairs, Benson. Tell the others to join us when they've done their stuff down here. You stay and see if you can get anything out of Mrs. Milner." The bulldog bared his teeth in a grin. "Young Waghorn, too, if you think he's worth the effort."

"He probably did it," said Stone as she prepared to follow her chief up the stairs. "Whatever it is. Waghorn, I mean. He's about the most least likely suspect so far . . ."

Neither Trewley nor Benson bothered to reply.

In the optician's private quarters the two detectives found hardly anything out of place. Only the still-burning lights—one in the hall, one in the bedside lamp—and the disordered state of the bedclothes struck a jarring note.

"No slippers," said Trewley. "No dressing gown. He'll have pulled 'em on when he heard the noise, I dare say."

"The instincts of the tidy-minded," murmured Stone as she examined Mr. Paine's small library of hardback books in the case at the foot of the bed. They were arranged alphabetically by author. "Once we've found him we could always ask him to pop into the station for a spot of freelance work on our files," she added with a faint sigh.

She straightened. She frowned. "If," she said slowly, "I were an elderly man chasing burglars in the middle of the night, I think I would take something with me. He didn't—doesn't—have a walking stick, does he?"

"Not the type to play golf, either," said Trewley. "Not what you'd call *physical* at all. He'd have a torch in case of power cuts, maybe. An organised bloke like him."

"Torch," said Stone, pointing. "Not really big enough to use as a weapon, though—but wait a minute, sir." She bent to study the cover of the book beside the bed. "*Thai Cookery*," she read. "Everyone needs a hobby, I suppose, but it gives me an idea. Shall we check in the kitchen?"

"That drawer," said Trewley as he followed her through the open kitchen door. "The only one not properly shut, and a burglar would've left all of 'em like that. Rolling pin, you reckon?"

"Instincts," said Stone again. "Yes, sir. Look at all the cookery books—oh." She had moved across to peer into the open drawer. "All those brown paper bags," she said slowly. "Folded nice and neat and flat . . ."

"Plastic carriers, too," said Trewley. His elbow nudged the handle of the cupboard under the sink. The door swung open: a flip-top lid was fastened to the inside. "Cheaper than bin liners," he remarked. "We do that as well."

"Snap," returned Stone absently. She stared again at the brown paper bags. "No names," she said, riffling with the tip of her pocketknife through the heap of folded bags to expose the surface of each in turn. "No printing," she enlarged as Trewley frowned at her. "Anonymous. And where in Allingham do you find the greatest concentration of plain brown paper bags, sir?"

"Ah," said Trewley, nodding. "I take it you don't mean the sex shop, Stone. Of course you don't," he added as her eyes narrowed dangerously. "Plain brown paper bags, cheap—the market," he said in triumph.

"The market," echoed Stone. "I wouldn't swear to it, of course, but I'll bet you a week's worth of sticky buns to a tub of low-fat spread that Mr. Paine was in the Market Square when they raided the Allshire and National Bank."

─── Twelve ───

YOUNG MR. WAGHORN was still in no state to have questions asked of him. Mrs. Milner, when questioned, thought for some moments before saying that on market days Mr. Paine, out of consideration for his staff, always took his lunch break much later than they did to give the morning rush of customers time to die down. Mr. Paine had indeed been in the Market Square when the Allshire and National Bank was raided: but so had a great many other people, most of whom had been far closer to the scene of the crime than he.

"Of course he was a little shaken by the experience," said Mrs. Milner. "As anyone might be," she added. "But he certainly didn't take it to extremes. He didn't make a song and dance about it." In the near distance Mr. Waghorn uttered a gentle moan.

"Did he give you the impression he'd recognised anyone?" Trewley pressed her as she fell silent. "Seen anything out of the ordinary? More than the robbery itself, I mean."

Mrs. Milner, having thought again, shook her head. "No, he didn't. And if you're wondering whether he might have remembered anything afterwards, I don't believe he did. He is a very conscientious man, Superintendent. He would have been in touch with you at once, I'm sure, if anything had come back to him. Goodness knows he was asked about it by enough people—customers—to have jogged his memory later, but as far as I know he didn't."

Her voice lifted in a slight interrogative note with her final words. Trewley nodded. "He didn't," he said.

"Then whatever has h-happened to him . . ." For the first time the admirable calm was shaken. Mrs. Milner took a deep breath and tried again. "Then this—this d-dreadful business must be merely a coincidence," she said, waving with one plump hand at the muted chaos of the stairway and its near surroundings. In the rest of the shop nothing had been found out of place by either the optician's staff or the police investigators. "A—a burglary—and poor, brave Mr. Paine interrupted them . . ."

Neither Trewley nor Stone could see why the burglars, whether interrupted or not, should wish to take Mr. Paine away with them as it appeared they had done: But they were careful not to voice that opinion aloud. Trewley spoke just ahead of Stone. "What do you keep in this place that's worth pinching, Mrs. Milner? You don't stock drugs—I won't believe you can get a buzz from eyedrops or polishing cloths—and my understanding is that one bloke's prescription would be useless to anyone else."

Mrs. Milner nodded. Trewley nodded back at her. "So they wouldn't want the glasses," he said. "And surely you don't keep overnight cash. Any shopkeeper with sense banks the takings at the end of each working day—and Mr. Paine strikes me as a bloke with plenty of sense. Besides," he added grimly, "most of the money's on credit card anyway, isn't it?" He could still recall the shock of finding the cost of the hated reading glasses on his monthly statement.

Mrs. Milner's neatly plucked eyebrows had lifted in discreet surprise halfway through this short speech. "I hate to contradict you, Superintendent," she said politely, "but we must have—oh, several tens of thousands of pounds tied up in our spectacles. Though not," she added as he stared, "in made-up prescription specs, that's true. Those, as you say, would be no use to anyone else unless he had identical eyes, which would be too much of a coincidence for anyone to swallow." She ignored the superintendent's automatic groan. "Nor," she went on, "is there much money in our

National Health glasses. But we do have a wide range of all the best-name designer frames in different sizes—and designer sunglasses as well. With summer only a few months away, and so many holidays abroad, Mr. Paine wanted to be sure . . ."

"Oh," said Trewley as she fell silent, pulling a handkerchief from her pocket to muffle a discreet sniff. "Oh," he said again, rubbing his chin and frowning. He was thinking of the news in that morning's paper; thinking of the stolen toothpaste, and of the young female optician who had been reported missing from Leeds . . .

A coincidence? Trewley didn't like them, but he knew he couldn't deny they happened. He thought of last week's bank raid and the likelihood of Mr. Paine's having witnessed more than he had remembered at the time . . .

"Thank you, Mrs. Milner," he said at last, rising to his feet with a nod. "We'll get back to the station now, if you'll excuse us. Constable Benson and the others will . . . see to things here. As soon as we have any news we'll let you know."

He had no idea how soon he would be called upon to honour that promise.

RETIRED HEADMASTER HORATIO Burley smoked a briar pipe, wore comfortable tweeds, and had a liking for the works of certain American humorists. His droop-eared, pert-nosed beagle cross had been named in honour of James Thurber; and not only by reason of his looks. Horatio would tell those who asked that the dog was naive, undomesticated, and without any breeding whatever, but that his sense of fun compensated for these minor flaws to make him an amusing, yes, and entertaining companion on the long nature rambles Mr. Burley so much enjoyed.

Thurber, tail wagging, dragged his master around the final street corner before Nirvana where the houses stopped, the countryside began, and the lead could be unclipped from his collar. The air was filled with tantalising scents borne on the first soft breeze of early spring. From the hedge came even more tantalising scuffles and squeaks. In the ditch oozed the rich, dark, aromatic mud in which Thurber loved to roll; in the distance gleamed the pond into which Horatio would coax him before they began their homeward journey.

They came to the stile and five-barred gate where their routine of disconnection took its normal course. Horatio stuffed the loosened lead in his pocket and climbed carefully on the hinge side up and over the gate: Stiles were for townies, and Horatio was country born and bred. Thurber flattened himself to his belly and squirmed his way underneath. Master and dog parted company on the far, free side of the hedge. Horatio took out matches and re-lit his pipe, leaning against that part of the gatepost he had over the years made his own. The weathered wood in that one spot was worn smooth and shining from the lazy weight of his body as, blowing contented smoke-rings into infinity, he contemplated in silence the peaceful view across the fields to the blue-hazed hills beyond.

The only sign of movement apart from the drifting smoky coils was Thurber, busily working his way along the hedge. Horatio had no fear for the safety of any small creatures the dog might meet. In three hopeful years Thurber had never succeeded in catching a thing, although one of the dog's predecessors had on two separate occasions been kicked by a doe rabbit, bold in defence of her kittens. Horatio blew a wistful smoke-ring and reflected fondly on the short, merry, loving lives of the many dogs he had owned. He remembered Seal, so named because of the surprising loudness of his bark when as a young pup he was accidentally locked in the spare bedroom. Thurber had arrived in time to share Seal's last six months . . .

Horatio sighed, clamped his teeth about his pipe, and was about to move on when he realised that it wasn't Seal who was barking in his reverie, but Thurber in real life.

"Come on, boy!" Mr. Burley didn't bother looking back: He knew the dog would follow once he had accepted that whatever shrew or vole he had disturbed had at least squatter's rights inside its burrow.

"Funny." Horatio paused halfway along the path across the field. Behind him, Thurber was still giving tongue in deep, rhythmic barks. By now he had usually given up on his vanished prey and come rushing after his master. "Thurber!" cried Horatio. "Here, boy! Thurber!"

Still the dog barked. He would have the neighbours complaining. Why anyone should move into a housing estate on the very edge of a town and then do nothing but grumble at the sights and smells—and sounds—of the country was a mystery to Horatio: but they had, and they did. He remembered how a pioneer householder—a city incomer who hadn't lasted long—had come ranting out of his sitting room to accuse Horatio's elderly spaniel Twain of leaving a decapitated pheasant in the middle of the front lawn. Twain's undoubted innocence had been briskly argued in an instructive discourse on the nature of the fox; the subsequent loan of a wildlife handbook had settled the fellow's hash nicely. He'd gone back to London, or wherever it was, and . . .

And Thurber was still barking. Horatio removed his pipe and put his fingers to his lips. He inhaled deeply, positioned his tongue, and let out a piercing whistle.

Thurber stopped barking. Horatio could see his white tail flag-wagging in the depths of the hedge. The dog did an energetic backwards shimmy and emerged to stand foursquare on the ploughed earth.

The dog threw up his head, opened his jaws, and howled.

Horatio Burley thought he had better go back and see what the matter might be.

Once he had seen, he went even farther back, to the nearest telephone, and summoned the police.

LESSER RANKS WERE still coning off the immediate area with fluorescent tape and portable screens when Trewley and Stone arrived. The superintendent was not a happy man, though the five-barred gate stood open now and nobody expected him to climb it. "I had a feeling this was coming," he said grimly as he led the way between the orange plastic guidelines.

"Yes, sir," returned the dutiful Stone. It was by no means the first time he had made the same observation since the telephone had rung in their office. She greeted her waiting colleagues with a nod but said nothing as, her hands in her pockets, she followed the superintendent to where the shadow of the hedge fell across the quiet, crumpled shape on the ground.

"Umph," said Trewley as he looked down at the body of a tall, thin, elderly man wearing blue paisley pyjamas and one leather slipper. The adhesive ring of a lost corn plaster glistened around the bony middle joint of the fifth toe on Mr. Paine's visible foot. His eyes, mercifully, were closed in his grey-white face. With another grunt the superintendent bent to peer at the neat indentations that marked either side of the aristocratic nose as if the man had worn glasses that didn't quite fit. "Shoemakers' children," he muttered as he straightened.

"Sorry, sir?" Stone generally contrived to follow the elliptical thought processes of her superior, but there were times when he could baffle even her quick wits.

"Shoemakers' children go without shoes . . ." Trewley's glance fell on the solitary leather slipper and the naked foot beside it. He cleared his throat. "Dressmakers' children go in rags," he continued sadly. "He took the time to make sure everyone's specs fitted properly . . . except his own, poor devil. That's Paine, all right." He sighed. "Poor devil," he said again.

"Yes, sir," said Stone, who had also recognised the optician. He had been a discreet but familiar figure around Allingham for many years.

"A pity, in a way, that Burley moved him. Still, you can't blame the man for wanting to make sure there was nothing he could do before he sent for us." Trewley turned his attention from that livid face—slumped sideways, mouth open in death—to the back of the corpse's head. "It's a bit of a mess," he warned his sergeant, who was trying not to look too closely. "He was hit several times by something pretty heavy, if you ask me."

Stone gulped. "Yes, sir," she said faintly, bracing herself to follow his example and finding that she couldn't. "His hands," she went on, in a rather more positive tone as she looked in another direction. "Wrists, that is. Those marks look to me as if he was tied up before he died, and . . ." She moved a cautious yard or so backwards. The sight of Mr. Paine's pale shanks exposed where the pyjama trousers had wrinkled, flesh and cloth both smeared with careless mud, seemed to Stone even more pathetic than the spectacle-pinches on the bridge of his elegant nose. She bent carefully down to study all she could see of the dead, white, wounded skin.

"Bound hand and foot," she said at last. "At his age!" It seemed a thoroughly inadequate comment, but she could think of nothing else.

"Poor devil," said Trewley for the third time. It was a far more suitable epitaph.

At this point in the proceedings they had to move aside to allow access to Dr. Watson. This much-bearded medico in self-defence carried in his wallet a photocopied list of every Holmes joke he had ever heard, and would hand it to anyone unwise enough to try another with the advice that saving breath made you live longer. He saw (he said) far too many people whose lives had been cut prematurely short to be able to approve of wasted breath.

Trewley and Stone waited, fidgeting, for five impatient minutes. At last . . .

"He's dead," said Dr. Watson, as required by law. Until this fact had been formally announced by a qualified medical specialist, no police investigation was, in theory, necessary. "Poor devil," he added, looking a little shaken. The professional contacts between doctors and opticians are not as close as those between doctor and doctor, but Mr. Paine had been, in a way, a colleague. "Killed elsewhere and brought here," he went on, doing his best to sound as impersonal as etiquette required. He almost succeeded. "Bruising suggests he could have been in a bit of a fight before they knocked him out. Mind you," he went on grimly, "at his age a fight wouldn't have lasted long. And—he wasn't a patient, so you'll have to wait to have this confirmed, but—from what I recall of the look of him pottering about the place, something tells me he may have had heart trouble. Do you know if he did?"

"No," growled Trewley, disturbed by a sudden vision of an elderly man hearing midnight noises and, reckless of his physical frailty, being brave—or foolhardy—enough to want to see for himself what was happening before calling for help. Had Paine, he wondered, had the time to call? It wasn't easy to imagine the quiet, well-spoken optician raising his voice even in an emergency, but . . .

"They hit him, then they tied him up." Dr. Watson was doing no more than confirm what had been already deduced. "Maybe while they decided what to do with him," he added. "Speculation's your end of the business, of course." He coughed. "But if you want my opinion, that bump on his head might well not have been necessary if they wanted to keep him quiet. The shock of getting out of bed to find the place crawling with desperadoes wouldn't have done the poor chap any good at all. And then with being tied up for some hours as he seems to have been . . ."

"Nasty," said Trewley, his bulldog features twisted in a disgusted grimace. Stone said nothing, though her silent look was equally eloquent.

Dr. Watson stood up and contemplated the hedge. He turned his head to gauge the distance between the body and the five-barred gate. "Well, it's your party again—but I'd say they didn't throw him over the top, they carried him here. And if you want an educated guess, 'they' might even have been—with all due deference to the good sergeant— 'he.' Poor Paine was tall, but there wasn't much of him. One man with enough muscle could have managed it—or two fit women," he added as he caught Stone's eye. "It isn't far," he pointed out, "and it's not as if it's heavy walking underfoot. When was the last time it rained?"

"We've already noticed he's left no tracks worth speaking of," growled Trewley. Stone said nothing.

"You'll be making enquiries about a car or van parked in the gateway, of course." Dr. Watson, now busy tidying away various instruments into his little black bag, chose not to see the expression that manifested itself on Trewley's face. The medical man needed some light relief as much as anyone. Paine had been a colleague . . . "Or how about a motorbike and sidecar?" Dr. Watson snapped shut the clasp of the bag and stood up, brushing the knees of his trousers and forcing a grin. "Or—since tracks would appear more conspicuous by their absence than by their presence—have you thought of a hot air balloon?"

"No," rumbled the bulldog.

"No," agreed the doctor. "Bruises not of a size to be consistent with being dropped from any height," he added as his mouth twisted inside the bushy black beard. "I'll leave you to it, then." And he was gone.

There followed a long silence. It was broken in the end by Trewley, who emitted a gusty sigh as with a thoughtful hand he rubbed his chin. "It's bad enough at the best of times," he rumbled sadly. "But when it's a bloke you know—knew, I mean—and when there's no rhyme or reason to it—the most harmless bloke you could hope to meet . . ."

"Yes, sir," said Stone. For a few minutes she had forgotten that it hadn't been only Dr. Watson who had known Mr. Paine in more than passing fashion. She tried for a lighter note. "Perhaps," she suggested, "we should look for someone he prescribed the wrong glasses for—someone who wanted to make a complaint and, um, got carried away. Or perhaps it was someone he advised to have bifocals. People can be touchy about these things." She ventured a sideways look at her superior, whose corrugated features were resolutely set. "Perhaps," she said in one last attempt to make him smile, "there really is a black market for contact lens cleaner—or for designer frames . . ."

"All right, Stone." He rubbed his chin once more. "All right. Point taken. This is a case like any other. Maybe it's connected to the bank business, but maybe it isn't." He frowned. "Maybe we should give the manager of Coates a friendly warning to keep an eye open in case anyone tries to break in over the next few days. They've tried two opticians so far, and been interrupted both times. They might," he concluded, "want to make it third time lucky."

─── Thirteen ───

ROBERT HERRICK, YOUTHFUL and enthusiastic manager of the Allingham branch of Coates, Opticians to the Nation, was a devotee of certain writings of Sir Arthur Conan Doyle. The magnifying glass on his blotter might have been no more than a professional tool, but the meerschaum beside it, and the deerstalker paperweight, were even more obvious clues to his obsession than the Sidney Paget original displayed behind antiglare glass in a gilded frame on the wall.

"Why, Superintendent, this is most gratifying!" Young Mr. Herrick rubbed his hands together and beamed. "It's the Red-Headed League all over again!"

Trewley, who hadn't read Sherlock Holmes since he was a boy, tried to make sense of this remark. What did Herrick know about the bank robbery connection that the police didn't? One of the clerks—the one who'd been shown in close-up in the Pearce news video—had been a redhead . . .

"The Allshire and National's only a hundred yards or so from here," went on Mr. Herrick, to Trewley's further bewilderment. "How many of your men will be on the stakeout? At what hour would you like to begin?" Then his face fell. "Sadly, I don't play bridge. But if you would be willing to consider cribbage an acceptable substitute—"

"Mr. Herrick!" cried Stone, as her superior could do no more than goggle. "This is a serious matter," she went on sternly. "You must remember, sir, that Mr. Paine was attacked, abducted, and killed by the very people we suspect may have designs on your shop." Mr. Herrick subsided meekly upon a chair. Stone tried to sound less stern and more reassuring now that the point had been made. "We haven't," she told him, "any actual proof they will break in, but there are definite grounds for suspicion. We think you should be aware of the possibility that they might." She shot a quick look at Trewley: who, relieved that his sergeant had taken charge, seemed disinclined to interrupt her. "As far as we know," she emphasised, "this has nothing whatever to do with the Allshire and National robbery—but someone was killed on that occasion, too, don't forget. We can't offer more than routine protection when we're so short of manpower with two serious cases on our books, but we can recommend a firm of security guards if your head office doesn't have a recognised policy for this type of occasion . . ."

They left Mr. Herrick babbling into the telephone, and made for the car. Trewley continued to say nothing all the way back to the station. Even the promise of iced buns and tea for two didn't bring him out of his apparent trance.

The reality did. He stirred a defiant spoonful of sugar into his mug and sipped. He bit into sticky dough and was restored. "Tell me," he begged through crumbs. "Was it me, or him?"

"I've a paperback copy I can lend you if you like," said Stone. "Don't worry about Herrick, sir. Some Sherlock fans can't distinguish fact from fiction. They write to him at 221B Baker Street—and sometimes they get an answer! Just imagine writing letters on behalf of a man who lived more than a hundred years ago to people who honestly believe he's still alive." She nodded to him over the top of her mug. "You and I have more important things to do, sir."

"Umph." Trewley took another bite of bun and sipped more tea. "I wonder if we ought to keep a watch on Coates, after all. I don't like coincidence. One optician might be just vandals, but two—and one of them murdered—is a bit more than that. Three . . ."

"We're not exactly up to strength at present," Stone reminded him. "Not with everyone busy house-to-housing

or checking statements, I mean. That's why we told Herrick
we couldn't do more than the usual drive-by, keep-an-eye-
on-things—and I don't realistically see how we can. Sir."

"*You* told him, you mean." Trewley scowled at his
paperknife in the old marmalade jar full of pencils. If a noise
woke *him* in the middle of the night, would he snatch up
even this feeble weapon in preference to wasting valuable
seconds going to the kitchen for a rolling pin? Until he was
in the same circumstance as Paine, it was impossible to
tell . . .

"You're right," he admitted after a grudging silence. He
hated to encourage her to get above herself, but murder—
even a hint of murder—was a serious business. "We can't
spare people for a stakeout, but we'll pass the word to the
panda crews to double back on their route when they go past
Coates whenever they can manage it." He brightened. "And
the place is alarmed to the station. We'll keep an extra eye
and ear open—when we can spare the time . . ."

But Tuesday night passed without any sign that anyone
had made even a halfhearted attempt to break into a single
Allshire branch of Coates, Opticians to the Nation. Trewley
had gone into overdrive and put out a general warning to the
county that mischief might be on the cards: Yet nothing had
been reported when he and Stone arrived at work on
Wednesday morning, and nothing was reported during the
next two hours.

"Hope the beggars haven't been scared off," growled the
superintendent as he dumped another batch of statements on
the Paine Murder heap and paused before tackling the latest
additions to the Bank Robbery file Stone had already
finished reading. "Wish we could have spared the manpower to do a proper stakeout job instead of relying on other
people. I'd love to feel their collars for the Paine business—
and the optician lead is the best we've got so far." He rubbed
his chin and scowled at the teetering pile of cardboard
folders. "Which isn't saying much."

"More's the pity." Stone, while waiting to swap paperwork with her superior, had been doodling on her blotter.
"He really does seem to have been Mr. Clean, doesn't he?"

"No children or family to get involved with undesirable elements and cause him any grief. A respectable widower—and no suspicious circumstances attached to the death of his wife. She'd been under the doctor's care for years."

"And everyone agrees that he did a wonderful job taking care of her at home for as long as he did," said Stone. "If it hadn't been for those awkward stairs, she would never have gone into the hospice at the end, I'm sure."

Trewley had removed the hated glasses and was squinting through them with alternate eyes. "Good at his job," he offered. "Thorough. Hard to think of him prescribing wrong and getting someone so upset they'd do anything more than take the specs back and ask to have 'em altered . . ." The superintendent set the glasses down on his blotter and frowned. "On the other hand, maybe he did. And maybe Hobson began to think he was costing 'em too much in replacements. Glasses," said the superintendent with a hint of bitterness, "are damned expensive things—well, the frames are. And the lenses not far behind, dammit."

"They can be way ahead," Stone told him, "if it's an unusual prescription. But even if he did make mistakes, they wouldn't have been wasted." Stone had eyes and used them. "Remember the collection bins? Most opticians have some sort of charity service for old frames and lenses and send them to deserving cases once they've been refurbished."

"Yes, of course." Trewley nodded. "Some of the prisons fix 'em in their workshops, don't they? It's a good scheme. Teaches the blighters to start thinking of other people for a change. Better than road signs," he added with a grin that showed his teeth. "Or mailbags, if anyone still does that. So if you're a poor old duck in a Third World country with wonky eyes that some lucky British bloke's castoffs will help, I'm all for it."

"As anyone with an ounce of public spirit in them would be," agreed Stone. "I honestly can't see Hobson's Choice getting hot and bothered over the odd astigmatic axis read the wrong way, if it ended up in a good home. But there's been no indication from anyone that Mr. Paine got things wrong at a more than average rate. If anything he was better than most, from what I gather."

"So they say." Trewley sighed, stretched, and grudgingly replaced his glasses as he reached for the Bank Robbery files. "We've been talking nonsense, girl. Never mind your brainstorming or whatever it's called: Let's get back to the good old-fashioned coppering I still say you can't beat. Method, routine, and common sense—they come through every time." He paused, rubbed his chin, and glared into the future. "In the end."

"Yes, sir," said Stone.

She didn't sound as if she believed it, either.

THEY ARE THE invisible people, conspicuous only by their absence. If they do a proper job of work, nobody pays compliment; if they cut corners or make a mistake, everyone complains. They are the unsung smoothers of life's untidy path: They are . . . the cleaners.

Invisible they might well be, but they are not always inaudible. When you linger too long at your office desk or spend too much time in your hotel suite, they lurk just outside the door to clash their buckets against the wall while shrieking romantic ballads at full off-key blast. And they pour streams of powerful disinfectant into the same buckets so that the air reeks with a fragrance to which their noses—and theirs alone—have become accustomed over the years. Should a hard-of-hearing smoker with a weakened sense of smell and the staying power of a limpet fail to be shifted by these means, they will retreat to the nearest window. This they open far enough to allow a draught, then they fling wide the limpet's door and plead innocent surprise as the paperwork—or the bedding—flies to all four corners of the room at once.

In hotels, motels, and guest houses the ubiquitous Do Not Disturb sign is the only way of keeping the cleaners out for more than a few hours. Honeymoon couples or those enjoying the illicit pleasures of the adulterous flesh are generously left to their own devices until the next day comes around. If the hotel, motel, or guest house is particularly busy the policy of discreet non-intervention might be extended by another twelve or even twenty-four hours before action is taken.

Forty-eight hours after the young couple had checked into Room 12A of the Allingham Arms and not been seen since, Mrs. Boyle knew that the time had come for action. Enough was enough. She took pride in her work. Was Room 12A to be left undusted and unpolished, its linen unlaundered, its carpets unhoovered, for as long as this? Access once a day was not unreasonable. Leave it too long, and the amount of catching-up she would have to do would play merry hell with her schedule for the rest of the week. Mrs. Boyle selected the biggest of the galvanised buckets and the most rattling of the trolleys in the cleaners' cupboard. For good measure she added half a dozen glass bottles of assorted domestic virtue and a small transistor radio with a dodgy aerial. Thus equipped, Mrs. Boyle began her cacophonous journey down the corridor where Room 12A was the only door to have been unopened for the past two days.

"Oops!" Mrs. Boyle tripped on a non-existent ruck in the fitted carpet and grabbed at the trolley for support. Its wheels locked briefly in a piercing squeal before it skidded sideways into the door of Room 12A.

The resulting racket had heads popping out of doors all the way up and down the corridor—except from the door of Room 12A. Mrs. Boyle frowned. She must be losing her touch. She switched on the radio and raised her tuneless voice to accompany the song being broadcast with one she made up as she went along.

Still nothing stirred behind the door of Room 12A. Mrs. Boyle sighed. With a great deal of rattling and banging she plucked the Do Not Disturb notice from the handle. Jingling sounds were followed by a clang as she dropped the passkey on its metal chain into the depths of the galvanised bucket.

"Cleaner!" cried Mrs. Boyle in desperation. She would never live this failure down. The Cleaners' Union imposed fines on those members who had to abandon subterfuge to get what they wanted. She might even have her ceremonial broom de-bristled if the Grand Mop was in a bad mood when the case was heard in chapter. Mrs. Boyle was in a bad mood herself as she inserted her passkey in the lock of Room 12A, gave the handle one last jangle, and opened the door.

"Cleaner!" cried Mrs. Boyle as she pushed the trolley inside and groped for the light switch. Curtains still shut at this time of day? "Rise and shine!" she instructed the sluggards. "Sorry to disturb you, but—"

Then she saw the figure in the corner of the room, and after a startled moment began to scream.

"SHE'S DEAD," SAID Dr. Watson, feeling more superfluous than he generally did in such circumstances. Medical qualifications were really not needed to be confident that in the blue-visage woman, whose eyes bulged above a gag that split her face in two, no vestige of breath remained.

"Suffocated," the doctor went on, as behind him the busy bustle of forensic activity kept Trewley and Stone temporarily from their work. "Been dead a couple of days, at a guess, though don't quote me until I've had a closer look."

"Bound, gagged, and female," mused Stone as she doodled in her notebook. "Kinky sex gone wrong, do you suppose?"

As the superintendent's face turned slowly purple, the doctor gave the matter serious consideration. "I wouldn't have thought so," he said at last. "You've got to be pretty damn kinked even to think of sex with someone wearing all her clothes, and there's no sign anyone's tried to take them off before he tied her up."

"And you'd have to be pretty damn athletic," supplied Stone with a mischievous glance at her superior, "if you're the one tied up and wearing the clothes and you, um, plan to take them off afterwards."

"Yes," said Dr. Watson. "She's physically normal, as far as I can tell. A little on the plump side, perhaps—not a keep-fit fanatic—but a contortionist, or anyone double-jointed, would have made quick work of the ropes around her wrists even if she couldn't manage the ankles."

Trewley's bulldog features had shaded from purple to

puce. He was determined not to mop his brow with his polka-dot handkerchief, but he knew it would be a close thing. "So you think—" he began, and coughed. He tried again as Dr. Watson and Detective Sergeant Stone politely turned their full attention upon him.

"So you think," he reiterated, "that . . . what's happened was entirely without her consent. And it happened some time on Wednesday. Umph. Whatever it was." He could not meet his sergeant's eye as he pursued this train of thought to its logical end. "Er—would you say she was conscious when it happened?"

Dr. Watson tugged at his beard. "She could have fainted—assuming it was an accident and not malice aforethought, that is—or she could have been doped when she was tied up. Which would certainly be malice, though not necessarily with intent to kill. Our party might just have wanted to keep her quiet for a while, and it went wrong. I don't think," he added, "that he knocked her out. There's no immediate sign of a bump on the head, though that yellow mop of hers is so thick, poor creature, I'd have to shave it to be sure."

Stone grimaced. She tried not to allow feminine considerations to affect her in working hours, but the idea of stripping the unknown of her crowning glory to satisfy the doctor's professional curiosity made her shiver.

"I hope she was doped," she said. "Or that she fainted. If she was in a—a nervous state to begin with, it might not have taken too long . . ."

"Yellow mop," muttered Trewley, whose own colour was returning to normal. "Yellow—Stone!"

"Yes, sir?"

"E. M. Forster!" barked the superintendent. The doctor blinked as Stone, after the briefest of pauses, nodded. A medico of literary tastes, Dr. Watson was less likely to connect the *Allingham Argus* with his rare periods of relaxation than *Howards End* or *A Passage to India*.

"Forster was chatted up in the pub by a—a buxom blonde a week or so ago," Trewley explained as Stone flipped to the front of her notebook and confirmed her suspicion that she had started another notebook during the

past week. "A complete stranger, he said. What's today—
Friday?"

"Yes, sir." They had been about to start their ritual shared
perusal of the local paper when the emergency call came
through.

"Exactly a week ago, then. The same day his piece about the
Allshire and National raid made front-page headlines." Trewley's brown eyes glittered as he began ticking off the points on
his fingers. "Blondie tried to pump him about it, he wasn't
playing, and someone knocked him out on his way home. And
when they let him out of hospital some beggar had turned his
place over, looking for something . . ."

"The register says the people had only been in Room 12A
a couple of days," offered Stone in her most respectful
Devil's Advocate voice.

Trewley dismissed the objection with a shrug. "Plenty of
hotels in Allingham," he reminded her. "What's to stop
her—them—moving every five minutes if they think
someone's after them?"

"If that's what they did, sir," said Stone. "And—if they
did—if that's why they did it."

Dr. Watson was tired of listening to detective theory when
he had preparations to make back at the morgue. "Then
you're going to have fun," he observed as he took his leave.
"First finding out who that poor girl is, then finding out
who's been on her trail, and wondering whether or not they
still are. And wondering," he added with a grin, "what's
happened to the chap who checked in with her. If he wasn't
the one who finished her off . . . Has the one who did
done the same to him?"

"Thank you, Doctor," said Superintendent Trewley.

Fourteen

THEY LEFT FORENSIC to finish whatever remained to be done in Room 12A and by mutual (though unspoken) consent, and with considerable (and likewise unvoiced) reluctance, made their way back to Reception. Trewley—who had politely offered Stone the lead, to have it as politely refused—did not hurry. There were some experiences against which even years of sparring with Desk Sergeant Pleate had not fortified the superintendent, whose memory was in some respects too good for his own peace of mind.

Stone, black belt in judo, had excellent reflexes. Despite this, she almost blundered into Trewley as he stopped in his tracks at the sight of the row of now empty deep armchairs. He blinked and stared again. Gone. The only remaining sign of life was (as he might have anticipated had he cared to consider the matter) behind the desk, where the lurking dragon—the grey-haired receptionist in the steel-framed glasses—banged down the telephone into which she had been speaking as the two detectives pushed open the door through which she had watched them vanish half an hour before.

"The Press," she informed the pair in tones of clipped distaste, though whether the distaste was for the Press or for the reappearance of the visitors whose arrival had so displeased her earlier, they could not tell. Her lips were forbidding, her eyes flint. The very ridges of her well-permed hair radiated complete self-control. "They will not be bothering us again."

At first Trewley wasn't so sure about that. On second thought, perhaps he was. From the first the receptionist had reminded him of nothing so much as a marble statue in a whalebone corset.

"Where's Mrs. Boyle?" he brought out, as with an arch of her well-plucked brows the receptionist silently enquired his business. He had thought to find the cleaning lady sitting over the cup of strong sweet tea he had suggested as a restorative. "I hope she's not too poorly. She hasn't gone home sick, has she? We'd like to talk to her again."

The receptionist looked past—looked straight through—the superintendent to his sergeant. Her brows arched again in a shared, unspoken *Men!* "Of course she hasn't gone home sick," said the receptionist aloud, in a voice as steely as her spectacle frames. "She is in the other wing." Trewley opened his mouth to ask for directions. She ignored him.

"Helping the other cleaner," she enlarged. Trewley's jaw dropped. With a gulp he forced it back again.

"Mrs. Boyle," said the receptionist, "has neither the time nor the inclination to be off sick." In anyone less dignified, this last might have been said to be accompanied by a sniff. "As well as being a most conscientious worker," the receptionist informed her visitor in withering accents, "she needs the money—and really, Superintendent, she is not so . . . feeble. Few of us are." From her tone it was unclear whether she meant few of those who worked at the Allingham Arms, or few of those who shared the same gender as her inflexible self. "Believe me," she went on, "when anyone has been in this business for as long as we have, it takes more than a body or two to unsettle us."

Again Trewley opened his mouth, and again he found himself shutting it. He was speechless.

Stone gulped. "Or . . . two?" she echoed after a pause. "You mean Mrs. Boyle has g-gone looking for another . . ." She gulped again. "For the man who checked in with her?" she concluded, then realised that this sounded ambiguous. "With the victim?" she amended.

"Mr. Leggett." The receptionist's voice was cold as she supplied this intelligence. "As far as I know, Sergeant, Mrs. Boyle has no particular reason to suppose that she might encounter the 'gentleman' in question during the course of her daily activities, which she has no intention of neglecting. It is more than improbable that Mr. Leggett will have been"—she winced—"invited to . . . conceal himself in any of the other rooms. Most of our guests are Regulars." The uppercase was very evident. "They know that I—that the Management—would strongly disapprove of anything that even hinted at"—she sniffed—"the unorthodox. As even in your line of work you must agree the despatch of a fellow guest should be considered."

Trewley remained speechless. "Y-yes," said Stone, quick to agree and marginally less intimidated than her superior. "But—but Mr. Leggett might have been hurt—or worse—in the same, um, incident as his wife. Even the best security measures can be circumvented if people try hard enough. And if an intruder had somehow managed to conceal himself on the premises—if he had been lying in wait for Mr. Leggett and—and silenced his wife almost by accident before attacking her husband . . ."

"If," said the receptionist darkly, "they were indeed husband and wife."

"Um. Yes. Um—have you any reason to suppose they weren't?" Stone was doing her best, but it was uphill work, with little or no support beyond the moral from her still-speechless superior.

"Mr.—and Mrs.—Leggett checked into their room on Tuesday afternoon," returned the receptionist, who had brought to perfection the art of the insulting pause. "And that was the last anyone saw of either of them. Until today." Both her tone and her expression did more than hint that she felt no further explanation was necessary.

Trewley felt his cheeks grow hot at the sudden gleam in his sergeant's eye. "Perhaps," ventured Stone, "they were on their honeymoon."

"Perhaps." The receptionist's thin smile acknowledged a

minor point. "At their age perhaps a second honeymoon—but in view of what has happened . . ."

"Yes," said Stone quickly. "Um—had either or both of the Leggetts stayed here on any previous occasion? With, um, anyone else?"

The receptionist, frowning, took a deep breath. Through his mental haze Trewley heard invisible whalebone creak. "I think not," she said. The hesitation had been minimal. "We tend not to encourage return visits from the more . . . flamboyant type of clientele." Pale lips primmed in the naked face. "This is a small, select, family operation. We would, I feel sure, have remembered . . ."

The receptionist's sallow cheek flushed an unhappy pink. Stone nodded. "You know everyone, and everyone knows you," she said, paying compliment. "But may *we* know how many of your clients during, let's say, the past week have not been regulars?" She was unable to bring herself to impart the obligatory uppercase inflection.

The sergeant had drifted up to the desk and was staring thoughtfully at the leather-bound register on which a firm but casual hand had been laid. No hint of polish tainted the neat, rounded nails. The hand was, for a moment, pressed more firmly on the leather cover before, with an audible sigh, the book was opened.

"I suppose," said the receptionist with obvious reluctance under Trewley's hopeful stare, "you will have to make a note of names and addresses. I—the Management—would appreciate it if you could try to disturb our Regulars no more than is absolutely necessary."

As Stone reached in dignified silence for her notebook, Trewley's conscience pricked him. He'd left the hard work to his sergeant for too long. "Don't worry," he said recklessly. "We'll make sure it's your casual customers who get the third degree first—umph." A glacial blast from those steel-rimmed eyes made him regret his words. "Umph. Yes. Carry on, Sergeant," he said weakly. "I'll, er, just check how they're all getting on . . ."

But it was through the front entrance of the Allingham

Arms and not back down the corridor in the direction of Room 12A that he beat a hasty retreat.

Ten minutes later Stone found him mopping his brow and brooding in the passenger seat of the police car. Startled, he almost brained himself on the car roof as she opened the driver's door and slid inside. "If I," Detective Sergeant Stone coldly informed her superior, "had done a bunk the way you did, there would have been a good many comments passed about women not being tough enough to take it. Sir."

He thrust his polka-dot handkerchief into his trouser pocket and sighed. "All girls together?" he offered, knowing how spineless it sounded.

Stone narrowed her eyes at him. "If you say so," she said after a noticeable pause. "As a matter of fact," she went on more cheerfully now that she'd made her point, "you might not have been so wrong, at that. Once you'd, um, gone on your way, she did rather unbutton." She brandished a slim sheaf of papers under his nose. "Two things, I think. For one, Leggett didn't have a credit card."

"Ah." Trewley sat up. "No wonder she thought he wasn't—they weren't—on the level."

Stone nodded. "He paid the deposit in cash. He didn't even offer them a cheque—"

"Untraceable." Trewley groaned. "Typical. Now we know he almost certainly was up to something, but we'll never be able to find the beggar to prove it."

Stone ignored his lament. "He paid cash," she repeated. "Sir." Something in her voice made him pay close attention. "Just like Mr. Black," she said.

Trewley scowled. "Who?"

"Black," said Stone, and once more brandished her prize too quickly for him to take proper notice. "If," she went on, "that was his name, which in the circumstances is open to doubt. He arrived an hour or so after the Leggetts on Tuesday and checked alone into a double room—and he's gone missing, too, sir. Without paying. No wonder she was in such a foul mood—"

"*Both* the beggars've done a bunk?"

"Not a sign of them anywhere."

Trewley rubbed his chin as he did swift calculations in his head. "Some time in the last forty-eight hours," he muttered. "And we've no idea when." Then he brightened. "This Black. Did he shove on a Do Not Disturb as well?"

"Evidently not, though the cleaner on that wing never saw him when she went into the room. I suppose he might have been bed-hopping with one of the other guests—it could just be a coincidence that he and Leggett—"

"No," barked Trewley.

Stone nodded. "No, sir." She coughed. "I took the liberty of asking Forensic to poke around his room just in case the odd fingerprint hadn't been polished away by Mrs. Boyle and Co. And I told Mrs. Boyle we'd be back later for a chat when she, um, wasn't so busy."

"Good girl." But Trewley didn't want her getting above herself. "And the second point?"

Stone's voice was tinged with mischief. "It seems that apart from his, um, fiscal arrangements there was nothing much out of the ordinary about Mr. Leggett, but Mrs. was quite another kettle of fish. Your friend on Reception didn't like her makeup, for instance."

"Flamboyant," quoted Trewley without bothering to answer the charge of friendship.

"Right." Stone was serious now. "Which suggests our dead Mrs. Leggett could well be the woman who was pumping Forster in the pub about the Allshire and National robbery." The sergeant brandished her papers again. "I told you she unbuttoned. She even switched on the photocopier for me! I've got all the guests for the past month. Naturally nobody who was here on Tuesday is staying here now—"

"Another blasted typical," snorted Trewley. For all his faith in good old-fashioned routine police work, he found knocking on unknown doors for the initial where-were-you-on-the-night-in-question stage of an investigation as boring as anyone else.

"Privilege of rank, sir." Stone knew her superior well. "We can farm this lot out to the beat boys while we go and unearth Forster from whatever watering hole he's decided to honour with his presence, and ask if he'd mind identifying the deceased for us. When it comes to coincidence, all this skirting around the Allshire and National edges is getting a bit much. We could really do with some hard facts—and once we know for certain she's the one, we'll have more to go on. Won't we?"

"I hope so," said Trewley, fastening his seat belt.

Stone took this as agreement and set the car in motion before he had time to propose using the radio to issue his instructions. She'd lost count of the number of times the repair shop had thrown up its collective hands in dismay at what happened when the superintendent and technology had a one-to-one encounter.

They detoured via the station and left the photocopied list with Sergeant Pleate. He made appropriate noises when told to assign uniformed officers to pursue enquiries, but maintained a resolute silence when informed by Stone that she and Mr. Trewley were off on a pub crawl. The desk sergeant's expression, however, was more than eloquent.

"I always think attack's the best form of defence," said Stone cheerfully as she buckled herself into the driving seat. "You should try it some time."

Trewley shuddered. "If I could've gagged you in time, I would have. We'll pay for this, my girl—mark my words."

"Think positive," she told him as she put the car in gear. "Where shall we go first?"

They decided that the redoubtable Forster was unlikely to have been deterred by a bump on the head and an overnight stay in hospital from patronising his usual pub: They were right, although out of luck.

"He was here half an hour ago," barmaid Tracy told them. "Then he got a phone call, and then he phoned someone else, and then he went."

Trewley glanced at Stone, Stone glanced at Trewley. The same thought had occurred to them both. Not-Much-Gets-Past-Me Forster could well have been the Press individual who had so much annoyed the receptionist neither of them had any great urge to confront again quite so soon . . .

"Duty calls, sir." Stone, resigned to her fate, did her best to sound bracing.

"We'll try the Trader first," weaselled Trewley. "Even if he manages to get past that—"

"Uh-huh." Stone raised a warning finger.

"Umph. Past that dragon," he amended. With a curt nod his sergeant accepted the designation. "Even if he makes it that far," he went on quickly, "Forensic will send him away with a flea in his ear. Most people end up in the Trader sooner or later. We'll try our luck."

And this time luck was with them. They even found a parking space on the asphalt forecourt of The Spice Trader, one of Allingham's favourite hostelries. "Ah, Superintendent! Sergeant Stone!" E. M. Forster was sitting at a corner table with a tumbler of dark golden fluid before him. He beckoned to the new arrivals. "There is villainy afoot," he informed them in a melodramatic whisper as they came within earshot. "Such monstrous villainy as our Tourist Board will find small inducement to strangers to visit our historic town, if not a veritable deterrent. Am I right?"

"Absolutely right." Trewley didn't ask how the reporter knew: He knew he would never be told. Good newshounds protect their sources. "And that's why we're here, sir. We'd like you, if you'd be so good, to take a look at the unfortunate lady to see if you recognise her."

E. M. Forster blinked at him. "I take it she's not still at the hotel," he said, pinching the end of his cigarette and preparing to put it behind his ear.

"We can give you a lift to the mortuary—when you've finished your drink," added Trewley. His tone implied that the finishing should not be too long delayed.

"Anything for our boys in blue," observed Forster as he raised his glass. "Begging your plainclothes pardon, that is. And yours in particular, Sergeant."

But Stone was too busy hoping that Trewley would not be tempted by the steak-and-kidney aroma coming from neighbouring tables, and the observation passed unanswered.

IN THE HOSPITAL mortuary the lingering ghosts of gravy, meat, and two veg were banished by the smell of disinfectant; the cheerful clatter of cutlery on china by the clink of clinical instruments on scrubbed ceramic tile. Memories of her student days sent a shiver down Stone's spine, and she took care to be at the back of the little group that approached the still, white-shrouded form that had only just been moved from the stainless-steel table to its last but one place of final rest.

"She'd been dead a couple of days before she was found," said Dr. Watson. "Died some time on Wednesday, at a guess. And she'd been doped for several days—enough to keep her quiet, not enough to knock her right out."

"Any more obvious abuse?" enquired Trewley as Stone shivered again and E. M. Forster muttered inaudibly.

"A few bruises, but nothing too serious. She was probably frightened—threatened, more likely—into swallowing whatever-it-was. The lab's still working on it. It appears she only managed a token resistance before it took effect." Dr. Watson echoed Trewley's sigh. "Poor creature," he said and led the way to the waiting white form.

"Ready?" he asked. Trewley and Forster nodded. Stone said nothing, and Dr. Watson did not ask again. He pulled back the cover from the corpse's head. E. M. Forster leaned forward.

"Yes," he said after a long pause. "That looks like her . . ." But he was frowning. He looked again. "Like," he muttered, "but unlike. I'm not sure . . ."

"She's not wearing makeup now," offered Stone from her position at the rear.

"Ah." Forster nodded. "Makeup. Yes." For the third time he studied the face beneath the pale golden waves of hair. "Makeup." He leaned forward, then back, and allowed his eyes to go in and out of focus.

"No," he said at last. "That's not the woman. I'm sure it's not. Mine was a blonde, and so is this one—but now I've thought about it, I'm absolutely sure. This woman is a complete and utter stranger."

─── Fifteen ───

THERE WAS A baffled silence.

Stone, venturing to take another peep at the dead unknown, frowned. Trewley rubbed his chin and scowled. Dr. Watson made to cover the corpse's head again.

The reporter shifted uncomfortably on his feet.

"You're not so sure after all, are you?" The challenge came from the doctor. The others remained silent.

E. M. Forster plucked the cigarette from behind his ear, muttered again, and thrust it back. "Yes," he said. "And no. This isn't the woman who chatted me up in the pub, I'm sure of that—but I'm not so sure she's a stranger. That is . . ." He closed his eyes. "I know her face," he said. "From somewhere. I think." He opened his eyes. "That white sheet . . . Black and white, that's how I see her. And I've seen her not so long ago . . ."

"In the papers," said Trewley.

"A photograph," said Stone, almost at the same time.

"A film star?" offered Dr. Watson. "A royal mistress?"

All three looked at him. Through the minds of the two detectives the same train of logic rushed in triumph to its destination.

A doctor. A dentist . . .

An optician.

"The missing optician from Leeds!" cried Trewley and Stone together.

•   •   •

THE ALLINGHAM ARMS receptionist was not happy at the third visitation. Her displeasure was made plain more by her manner towards the two detectives than by her actual words, which were as genteelly firm as ever, with the emphasis being very much on "firm." She refused to abandon her post. She saw no reason to disturb the Management by asking for alternative arrangements to be made for the acceptance of bookings, the welcome of guests, the farewell to same, and the clearance of their cheques and credit cards. Cash, it was evident to Trewley and Stone, was no longer sanctioned by the Management—or by the receptionist—as a method of payment at the Allingham Arms.

"The notes," they were told, "might be forgeries." And that was that. There was, very noticeably, no mention of the distasteful events to have followed upon the last cash transaction to have taken place at the hotel.

No, she did not care to interrupt Mrs. Boyle's cleaning routine for the second time that day when the woman had, after all, only ever seen the so-called Mrs. Leggett once before—and that when she was dead.

"Except," said Trewley, "that we don't believe she did. That she is. Was, I mean. See her, necessarily. The same woman, that is." Only his fear of what Stone might afterwards say stopped him groping in his pocket for his handkerchief, though his brow was steaming. "The same as you," he concluded, feeling a fool. If the woman hadn't reminded him so powerfully of one of his old school-teachers . . .

"I?" The receptionist's eyebrows arched to her hairline. "I saw her once, when they checked in on Wednesday. I really would not care to commit myself to an identification, Superintendent. My main impression is of far too much makeup and of hair that was probably"—and here she sniffed—"peroxide."

Stone shifted beside her superior. Another woman would notice, when a man would not. Forster had at first thought Yes, then No . . . It made sense.

"Thank you," she said. Trewley looked at her. "You've

been most helpful," she went on. "If we need you again, we know where to find you—don't we, sir?"

He'd trusted her more than once before this. "Yes," he said, without demanding immediate answers to the various unasked questions that would certainly be asked once the two of them were somewhere private. "Yes," he said again with more confidence. "Thank you, madam. Good afternoon. Come along, Sergeant."

Outside on the step, before the main door had clicked properly shut behind them, he turned to her. "Peroxide?"

"We can radio Doc Watson from the car," she said, throwing caution to the winds and the repair shop. "But I think our body is—was—a natural blonde, sir. Which means . . ."

"Two different women," said Trewley. "So Forster was right." For the second time that day he stopped in his tracks, and Stone almost bumped into him. "Two different women," he said again. "Which means, dammit—there's now three people missing we've got to find!"

THE PRELIMINARY SCENE-of-the-crime report was waiting for them when they finally reached the station. Trewley issued instructions that word should be passed to the North of England force that their missing woman might well be in the Allingham morgue, and that an exchange of fingerprints by fax should settle the matter. While files were duly searched and telephone wires prepared to hum, he and Stone settled to a detailed study of documents that even for a murder investigation were of considerable interest.

After five minutes Trewley took off his spectacles and blinked. He blinked again. The typewritten letters did not move. "*Three* bottles of contact lens cleaner?" he demanded, jabbing a finger on the second sheet of paper on his desk. Stone, whose eyes were happier with close detail than those of her longsighted superior, looked up from the photographs that were her share of the checking.

"Unopened," the superintendent added darkly. Without a word his sergeant picked up the telephone. There were some things she did not need to have spelled out to her.

"Hello, Doctor." The wait until the medico could be retrieved from wherever he had been working had seemed like an age to both Stone, clutching a voiceless handset, and Trewley, trying with poor success to concentrate on the other listed contents of the hotel room.

"You and I really must try to stop meeting like this, Sergeant." Dr. Watson's laugh was almost deafening. "What is it now? Should you have continued to agonise in private over whether or not our most recent acquisition is wearing a wig, let me assure you again that she is not."

"It's nothing to do with her hair this time." Stone had been but marginally more amused than her superior—who had not been amused at all—by some of the doctor's previous remarks on the subject of wigs and where they could be worn by persons of either gender. Allingham police cars had not yet been fitted with radio scramblers, and there were members of the public who listened to constabulary frequencies on a regular basis. "*Nothing* to do with her hair," reiterated Stone. "Although it is," she conceded, "to do with her appearance. Did she wear contact lenses?"

"Good heavens." Dr. Watson was for once dumbstruck. Only ten seconds later did he manage to reply. "She didn't when I last looked," he said. "Mind you, I couldn't take my oath she didn't wear 'em on and off—for special occasions, say, and with glasses for day-to-day—but there were no indications that she wore glasses as a regular thing either, come to that."

"Or if she did," said Stone, thinking of the pinch-marks on the nose of Mr. Paine, "they were a perfect fit."

"She didn't," growled Trewley, who—having struggled to the end of the Contents list and had his suspicions confirmed—was on the other phone. "Not a pair of specs in the place, and no sign of contact lenses either. Apart from *three* blasted bottles of cleaner. Same brand. Doc, this may sound daft, but is it possible to —to get a buzz from contact lens cleaner?"

"Daft?" echoed the doctor. "Ha! Some idiots can inject almost anything into themselves and think they enjoy the sensation. Remember those wild tales about salad dressing years ago? Mind over matter, if you ask me."

"Except that if they'd had minds they'd have used them," Trewley growled. "Same as nowadays. Anyone with brains isn't drugging at all—with anything."

Thus brought back to the point, the doctor thought for a moment or two. "I can't see how you could," he said. "Not realistically. It isn't as if it's alcohol based, the way gripe water used to be. All those teething babies neglected because their mothers got a taste for the stuff—but contact lens solution? You'd better talk to one of the local opticians, but for what it's worth, I doubt it."

"So why," demanded Trewley once the call was over, "does anyone who doesn't need it have *three bottles* in her room? They aren't Leggett's or his wife's or whoever our peroxide mystery woman is. They didn't wear contact lenses. There's no mention on this list of a case to keep 'em in."

"They might be the wear-them-a-week-and-throw-them-away type," said Stone. "But even then whoever wore them would have a spare set for emergencies, wouldn't they? Unless they came away in too much of a hurry to pack."

"They had time to kidnap the woman," said Trewley. "She was no willing accomplice, I'll swear. You don't dope the people on the same side as you—and dope doesn't grow on trees. They'd have to pinch it or fiddle a prescription or buy it from someone or—or something. Now, anyone that well organised doesn't forget what makes it possible for him—or her—to see what they're doing. Moreover, Detective Sergeant Stone, if they were the throwaway sort, he wouldn't need cleaner at all." Only when he believed he had scored a point did the superintendent ever address her in full.

"Not that I know much about it," he added as she smiled faintly. "I've never liked the idea of putting things in my eyes, although . . ." With a jaundiced glare he contemplated the spectacles lying on the blotter. "But I suppose you can't help hearing about 'em . . ."

Slowly she nodded. "Three unopened bottles," she said in a thoughtful voice. "Is that all it says?"

"Why?" His tone was sharp. "Hyaline brand, it says. The small size."

"Just a minute." She shuffled through the photographs again. "Yes, this one—wait—yes." She fished around for her magnifying glass, bent low, and peered for a moment. "I thought so," she said. "Look, sir."

She handed him a close-up shot of the bedside shelf on which stood a reading lamp, an unused ashtray, a telephone, and other impersonal hotel paraphernalia. It was a double shelf, deep enough to hold not only a telephone directory out of focus at the back, but also, in front, three bottles. These were all the same size and shape and, though facing in different directions, all—according to the one legible manufacturer's label—held Hyaline Lens Solution.

But the size, shape, and colour of two of the three price labels were obviously not the same. Trewley, squinting through her magnifying glass at the third bottle, could—like his sergeant—guess the appearance of the price label out of shot.

"Three different opticians," said the superintendent, and Stone did not disagree, "or I'm a Dutchman." Which he most certainly was not. "Three *local* opticians," he added. "Eye Deal here." He jabbed a finger on the photograph. "Coates. And what's the betting this one says Hobson? I'll send someone back to the hotel to check. Why the devil they didn't write it down in the first place . . ."

Stone ignored his complaint. She was thinking aloud. "If the bottles had come from the same shop, we could argue that Leggett, or whoever, was—was keen on the assistant and needed an excuse to keep going there. But *different* shops . . . The excuse idea still holds, but not the reason for it. Unless," a hint of mischief made her add, "he has a fixation of some sort. Sexual deviation takes many forms— though I think it's unlikely in this instance," she added as her superior began to turn purple. It wasn't fair to tease him further: Dr. Watson had already upset him quite enough.

"Casing the joint," she said hurriedly. "That's what he'll have been doing, sir. But—why?"

Trewley looked at her with guarded approval. "We'll go and ask—No, we won't. We'll check those break-in reports first." He rubbed his chin and favoured the filing cabinet with a contemplative stare. "We know only too well what happened at Hobson's . . . Coates haven't been in touch at all . . ." His bloodhound gloom was lightened by a sudden grin. "That Herrick bloke—the Sherlock Holmes freak who kept babbling about red hair—he would've been on to us like a shot if he'd found the slightest excuse, wouldn't he?"

Stone, who had jumped to her feet at his earlier words and was busy rummaging through the middle drawer of the tall steel cabinet, had to agree that he would. Trewley nodded. "And Miss Eye Deal said nothing had been taken, didn't she?" he went on. "As far as she knew. I think." He frowned.

"I think so, too," said Stone, who had pulled out a cardboard folder and was leafing briskly through the contents. "Benson . . ." she murmured to herself. "As far as she knew," she confirmed after a few minutes. "But you can't help wondering, can you?"

Trewley had been studying his scene-of-crime list again. "Three pairs of rubber gloves," he said slowly. "What do you make of that? And," he warned, "I don't want any jokes about—about kinky sex in double rooms, please."

Stone saw that he was turning purple again. "No, sir," she said, mouse-meek. "Well," she went on brightly, "unless the Leggetts were the sort of people who only wear them once and throw them away—"

"They weren't in the wastepaper basket," Trewley told her. "Only the wrappers." He invested this last with a dark significance that for the moment passed her by.

"New, then," she said. "And bought especially for . . . some purpose we don't yet know. But—"

"Even money says it's fingerprints," interposed Trewley before she could beat him to it.

"Well—discounting, um, kinky sex—yes, sir, I agree. I suppose it would be too much to hope for price labels." She shot him a wary look. She had no idea how far domesticity was currently imposed upon her superior by his spouse and daughters. "Of course, most supermarkets now have bar codes and electronic scanners," she said, as if reminding him of what he already knew. "They seldom label individual items unless they're on special offer, and not always then. But a supermarket is where I would go to buy . . . anything I didn't want to have people remember me buying and talk about afterwards. I doubt if we'll trace them that way."

"My wife," remarked the superintendent in a thoughtful voice, "buys rubber gloves half a dozen pairs at a time." Before Stone could comment, he made the big confession. "In two sizes. I can wash a dish with the best of 'em, Stone."

"I'm delighted to hear it, sir."

"Umph. Well, that's as may be. But I hope you're not saying you'd start suspecting her—or anyone else with more than themselves to shop for—of heavens knows what if you happened to get stuck behind 'em in the queue and spotted what was in the trolley."

She smiled. "It wouldn't surprise me if Mr. Herrick went into deduction overdrive, but for myself I'd be rather less, um, romantic in my suspicions. You're right, lots of people buy more than one pair at a time, in case they perish or puncture too quickly. Only—three pairs of rubber gloves? For two people supposedly on holiday? No, it has to be fingerprints."

"Four people," Trewley corrected her, his voice darkening once more. "And . . . not on holiday. Up to something, otherwise why the gloves? Four people, and three pairs of gloves . . . Nasty."

Stone shivered at the unspoken horror behind that simple statement, but said nothing. "Four people," said Trewley again. "One forcibly restrained, probably kidnapped, and now dead—and three disappeared."

Once more she said nothing. Once more she was thinking; and her thoughts were not pleasant. The superintendent, understanding that her silence was not rudeness, likewise was silent. For over two minutes neither of them spoke.

"We don't *know*," said Stone, "that our body is the missing optician. Not yet. Not for certain."

"It's a damned funny coincidence if she isn't, Stone."

"Yes . . . They're taking an age to check their records." She was finding it hard to sit still. She fished among the documents on the superintendent's desk. "Coincidence," she said, half to herself. "What we *do* know is that the prints we have here are the prints of the murder victim—one of the murder victims, I mean." She opened a cardboard folder and stared again at the two rows of five fat, lined ovals. "I wonder . . ."

"We ought to check with all three shops that these are their labels," Trewley said. "And check that Doc Watson's right the stuff isn't—isn't addictive."

"They might even remember who bought the bottles," said Stone, who didn't for a moment believe it, but who was as keen as Trewley for action of some sort.

"We'll go and talk to them," said Trewley. He pushed back his chair, rose to his feet—and hesitated as Stone, in the act of reaching for her jacket and keys, herself hesitated to take one last look at those fat, lined ovals with their loops and whorls and spirals.

The superintendent watched her. "Fancy a refresher course, do you?" he barked, and a slow smile spread over the face of his subordinate.

"Two minds with but a single thought," said Detective Sergeant Stone.

Sixteen

"Your glasses, sir!" Stone, glancing over her shoulder, stopped in the doorway and called out the reminder to her superior's disappearing form. "If you're—we're—going to be looking closely at things . . ."

"Umph." Trewley had been halfway down the corridor in his eagerness to be away. He shrugged, sighed, and stumped back into the office to snatch the offending spectacles from his blotter.

He put them down again. "Lost the case," he muttered as he caught Stone's eye. "Don't want to risk scratching the blessed things, the amount they cost. I'll do without."

She said nothing, but she said it with some eloquence.

"Look," he said. "If I can't make out the—the odd detail the shop can always lend me a magnifying glass, can't they? Or a pair of those cheap off-the-peg specs you can choose for yourself. I'll manage."

Still she said nothing, as eloquently as before.

"Oh, come on," said the superintendent. "It's my problem, not yours. I get enough nagging at home about wearing the damn things. I don't need it here."

"It's your choice, sir." Stone was prim. "If you are prepared to take the risk that there will be a suitable—"

She broke off. She stood with her mouth open. Slowly, without a word, she closed it. Trewley stared at her. As he in turn opened his mouth to ask what was wrong, she shook her head. She gazed at him blankly for a moment, then shifted her gaze from the familiar corrugated face to the pink, bespectacled blotter on his desk. She moved to the desk and picked up the glasses, holding them at arms' length, twisting them to and fro as she peered through them first at the window frame, then at the door.

"The vertical doesn't stay vertical," she muttered. "The right, anyway. Left seems okay . . ."

She peered and twisted some more. Satisfied at last, she nodded and handed the glasses to their owner. "You try," she said. "Hold them out the way I did and keep your eyes on a straight line, like the edge of the door—and twist them about—but don't lose sight of the line. What happens?"

Trewley followed her instructions. Halfway through a twist, he grunted. "Line wobbles," he said. "Well, the right one does. The left stays the same. What's so exciting about that?"

"You're slightly astigmatic in your right eye," she told him. He looked at her and lowered his arm from the horizontal line-checking position to the normal.

"I know," he said, replacing his glasses on the blotter and trying to stay calm. "I'd forgotten the exact word, but I knew it was something similar—but is that a reason for you to go temperamental on me? It's not catching. It's not that unusual, for heaven's sake. Don't *fuss*. You're behaving like a—a wife instead of a police officer, dammit."

"With due respect, sir, I'm behaving like a detective." Stone picked up the despised spectacles and brandished them under her superior's nose. "The combination of the astigmatism and your prescription means that—like a lot of people who wear specs—you wouldn't find it all that easy to wear an off-the-peg pair for any length of time without feeling . . . uncomfortable. A headache, probably. Perhaps a stiff neck and shoulders as you tense your muscles to compensate for the faulty message your brain's been receiving from your eyes—"

"For heaven's sake!" This time it was a cry of exasperation. "I know all that! I don't need a health lecture, Stone. It'll be my blasted diet next, or my blood pressure—which you and your nonsense are making a damn sight worse than it would be if you'd only . . ."

He stopped. He stared at her. He looked at his glasses and, after a moment, took them from her unresisting hand. He held them at arms' length and twisted. "He did say," he muttered, "that nobody ought to wear anyone else's specs and that with some people it mattered more than others . . ."

Still holding the glasses, he grinned. "Sorry," he said. "I think I see what you're getting at."

Stone grinned back at him. "So you do, sir," she said, with a nod for the glasses. "Your case," she added gently, "is in the top left-hand drawer, I expect. Where you, um, usually leave it. You'll be wanting to bring them with you after all, won't you? Sir," she ended, and whisked out of the room before he could say another word.

"IT'S A PRETTY wild guess," he observed as the police car rumbled into the road leading to the high street. It was the first time either of them had spoken since Stone turned the key in the ignition.

"It's the best bet so far, isn't it?" She slowed for a corner, extra careful at this time on a Friday afternoon when office workers eager to begin their weekend were hurrying home with more enthusiasm than sense. "I mean, sir, we've had coincidence after coincidence—and you know how you enjoy them—and there are just *too many* opticians in all this. They have to mean something—something special. And if someone's prescription isn't special—unique—then I don't know what is."

"A dentist can mess about with teeth," he said, playing the Devil's Advocate role she generally took for her own. "Crowns, bridges, plates, and screws, take 'em out and move around what's left—my eldest had it, and I know. So why not an optician with eyes? I've heard—read—about laser beams and all the technology." He shuddered. "Can't say I fancy it myself, but then I wouldn't want contact lenses. Not everyone's like me, though. Models—

actresses—women are tougher than men, Stone, when it comes to their looks."

"Ah, yes, we must suffer to be beautiful." Stone sighed artistically. "How glad I am to be nothing out of the ordinary in the looks department. But be fair, sir. There are quite as many vain men as there are women—and often there are practical, even medical, reasons for having surgery. Or contacts. Though not as often as teeth," she added.

"The best bet so far," he said, echoing her own words. "But it's still a pretty wild guess . . ."

In a thoughtful silence the car continued its journey towards the Allingham branch of Hobson's Choice, Opticians.

Matronly Mrs. Milner was ushering a customer out of the shop as Stone—at this time in the afternoon prepared to risk the wrath of the traffic wardens—pulled the car into the kerb an politely pipped the horn before switching off the engine. The optician's tweeded assistant looked across, recognised her visitors, and waved.

"You were lucky to catch me," Mrs. Milner told them as they made their way inside. "I've a dentist's appointment in half an hour and I was closing early. Young Waghorn has been off sick since poor Mr. Paine . . ."

Mrs. Milner stifled a sob. "Mr. Hobson," she said, rallying, "has found us a qualified locum for market days and Saturdays, but I'm afraid I am able to do no more during the rest of the week than sell disposables and adjust earpieces and advise anyone who wants a new set of frames with an old prescription." She missed the quick and meaningful glances exchanged between Trewley and Stone at her final words. "I do hate," she said apologetically, "to sound uncooperative. But is whatever you want going to take long?"

Trewley replied in a matter-of-fact tone. "That depends on whether you trust me and my sergeant to lock the place up for you after we've done. We'll be as careful as you like, and we can drop your keys off at your house later on if you tell us where you live—but we can't say how much later as we don't know how long it will take."

"It?" echoed Mrs. Milner, puzzled. "Not wishing to be rude, Superintendent, but what?"

Trewley shook his head. "I'd prefer not to go into details, Mrs. Milner. Let's just say something's come up we'd like to investigate further. A few more checks, if that's all right by you."

As he spoke, Mrs. Milner had gone pale. Her gaze shot up to the now empty flat above the shop. "You mean you think somebody might be going to—to attack me or Richard next?" The words came out in an unsteady voice, and she sat down quickly on one of the easy chairs by the window.

Stone, glaring at her superior, sat down just as quickly on the neighbouring chair. "No, we don't," she said firmly. "In fact, it may sound callous to say so, but it's *because* poor Mr. Paine was . . . attacked that we can be pretty certain you aren't in any danger. Unless your dentist goes mad with the drill," she added. "Or fills the wrong tooth, or spills that horrible pink mouthwash they all seem to use down the front of your best dress . . ."

At this, Mrs. Milner achieved a faint smile and became more like herself. Stone smiled back. "Honestly," she said, "this is just a—a cross-reference, if you like." She looked at Trewley, but he was not signalling her to be silent. "We believe," she went on, "that if Mr. Paine's attackers hadn't—done what they needed to do, they would have been back by now."

Still Trewley said nothing. "We think," said Stone, "that it might not have been designer frames they were after—and we want to make sure." She achieved a martyred sigh. "And if you can show us where you keep your vacuum cleaner and so on, we'll be only too happy to, um, dust everything before we go. Won't we, sir?"

Her superior recalled his confession on the matter of dishwashing, and groaned cheerfully. "I'm sorry to say my sergeant's right, Mrs. Milner. A spot of powder from the fingerprinting, that's all there'll be—and of course we already have yours and young Waghorn's, so there's no need to keep you any longer. I'm sure you can't wait to get to the dentist."

Mrs. Milner had gasped at his mention of fingerprints. "You mean you think," she said weakly, "that—that I—or Mr. Waghorn—or one of—of our clients might have k-killed Mr. Paine? But—"

"No," chorused Trewley and Stone. The superintendent bent low to pat Mrs. Milner's shoulder, which shook despite her best efforts at self-control. "We can trust you to keep a confidence, I'm sure," he said. "As I told you, we have good reason to believe there's more behind Mr. Paine's death than we suspected at first, but we do need to be sure of our facts. And we've a shrewd idea that going over the shop in, uh, rather more detail than we did before might just give us those facts."

The reiteration gave nothing away, but sounded impressive, though not as reassuring as he'd intended. Mrs. Milner was puzzled but trusting. "If you say so," she said doubtfully. "You all seemed so very thorough when you were here last time—but . . ."

She coughed. "Of course," she said in a voice that was almost level. "Mr. Paine's death was a great shock. Everyone liked him so much, and I want to do what I can to—to catch . . ." She cleared her throat. "Yes. Yes, please help yourselves. Here are my keys. You'll be sure to lock up, won't you?"

Ten minutes later the Closed sign hung on the door, the blinds were down, and Trewley and Stone were at the rear of the shop preparing to wrest what secrets they could from the depths of the Hobson filing system.

"Poor visibility from the road," Stone pointed out as she unpacked her gear. "That'll be why whoever it was had to come right inside and buy something like contact lens solution rather than just peer through the window."

Trewley grunted. Before leaving for the dentist, Mrs. Milner had told them where the cleaning equipment was kept. In the superintendent's opinion, a mere sergeant had no business presenting him with a fluffy pink nylon duster on a stick together with a heavy hint that he would be called upon to do his share. He wouldn't have minded quite so much if the thing had only been blue.

"Cheer up, sir." Stone was ready to start work. "With any luck it will all be over by Christmas—and I think I can fly this thing," she added quickly, pulling open the top drawer of the filing cabinet and gazing inside. "Personal records," she went on, "are pretty basic. When you think of some of the paperwork we've had to wade through in our time, this lot shouldn't cause us any problems."

He loomed over her shoulder to see if she was being unduly optimistic. "Alphabetical by surname," he observed in an irritable tone. "Oh, yes, fine if you're called Aardvark—but why doesn't someone, just once in a while, start with—with Zodiac. Or Zulu?"

"Zedabetical," Stone told him as she turned to pick up a pair of slender yet sturdy tongs. "That's what I've heard it's called. The opposite of alphabetical."

"Zedabetical," repeated Trewley, trying out the new word with his ballpoint on a pad of lined paper. "Zedabetical. Now I like the idea of that."

"Oh, I can sympathise," she said, brandishing the tongs. "I'm almost as badly off as you, remember—but then what would happen to people called . . . Myxomatosis? Or Nabob? They would never have their chance to be first. They'd always be in the middle."

"Good old British compromise," said Trewley, then fell silent, watching, as with her tongs she carefully removed a buff card folder of a pocket, or upright wallet, design from the front of the drawer and put it on the table.

"Abbott, Clemency," said Stone. "Two bees, two tees."

Trewley crossed out "zedabetical" and wrote down the name on his pad.

"Thank goodness it's the shinier type of cardboard," his sergeant went on after dictating Clemency's address and date of birth. "Calendared, isn't that the word? A more uneven surface would have been a nightmare."

"Nice and new," observed Trewley as he fiddled with the cable of the small but powerful electric-light box he had been instructed to plug into a suitable socket. Stone was willing to trust him so far, but no farther. Well, he'd never claimed to be one of your technical-minded blokes. "Young

Hobson's done us proud with his modernising," he went on. "Maybe we're going to be in luck after all."

"Let's hope so," replied Stone, carefully brushing the smooth surface of the wallet with—in view of her promise to Mrs. Milner—no more than enough aluminium powder to disclose what there was to be disclosed. "Yes," she said as she put down her brush. "Most of them are reasonably clear. Good . . ."

Delicately she rolled transparent sticky-tape over one print at a time, folded it double, and set it to one side. When each of the prints had been lifted in this way she used the tongs to turn the folder over and repeat the process. Trewley tried not to tell her to hurry up. He knew she was doing a better job than he could ever manage.

"*Very* good," she murmured as the last piece of tape was folded. She reached across for the magnifying glass. Without a word the superintendent placed it in her hand, switched on the light box, and waited.

"Thanks," she murmured, peering at the prints one after the other against the white background. "Yes," she said at last. "These are Waghorn, nearly all of them—and a few Milner—and some smudges around the top that with the best will in the world I can't identify."

"Apprentice," said Trewley. "You know what I mean," he added quickly as she prepared to be affronted. "Young Waghorn. Beginners are allowed to do only the boring work till everyone knows they can be trusted. Filing and so on."

"Necessary routine work," came the polite correction. "Talking of which, sir, here you are." Gravely Stone handed Abbott, Clemency to her superior and turned away to remove the wallet for Jonathan of that ilk.

"Mother and son," said the superintendent as he wrote to her dictation. "Same address, right sort of age difference with her being . . ." In the Hobson system only name, address, and date of birth were given on the front of the folder. He did swift calculations in his head as he applied his duster to Clemency's file. "Thirty-two," he said.

"Our Jonny must have had a check-up recently," deduced

Stone after a while. "See how Mr. Paine's prints are on top of Richard Waghorn's?"

"Nobody else?" Trewley, waiting to exchange Clemency for Jonathan, was growing restless.

"One Milner, more smudges at the top. As if someone had riffled through the files without pulling them out—which is what happens, of course. You never seem to go straight to the one you want. I've noticed that before."

"Well, Abbott's way up the alphabet," said Trewley. "At the front of the drawer. You couldn't hope to see what was behind without moving—touching—the tops of the files at least. With or without gloves," he couldn't help adding.

"Four people," said Stone, who felt that if he couldn't be hopeful, she had to hope for both of them. "Three pairs of gloves. Remember, sir?"

"Umph," was all Trewley said, though he glared at the wallet Stone still held as if Jonathan Abbott were personally to blame for the superintendent's gloom.

"I wonder," muttered Stone. She, too, contemplated Jonathan in silence for a moment or two. "He's only twelve," she said, half to herself. "And I have to practise on someone." With finger-tips and thumb she squeezed the sides of the wallet, which bulged open just far enough for her to insert a cautious tong tip and pull out the card. This she laid flat on the table; then, using the "magnetic flake" brush from her bag, she dusted powder from a different container over the card's surface, crossed mental fingers, and reached for the camera. "Close focus," she said to herself, and pressed the shutter.

Trewley blinked at the flash and began grumbling almost immediately. As he fretted for the film to develop, Stone, trying to ignore him, powdered the next wallet, that of Abbott, Amanda Jane, who lived at the same address as Clemency and Jonathan. Neither detective could decide whether the girl's out-of-sequence position was careless filing on the part of the Hobson staff or something more sinister, but the sticky-tape stage of the investigation had to wait as, with a click and a *whirr*, the film of the Jonathan prints emerged from the camera.

Stone studied it through the magnifying glass. "Paine," she said at last. "Several times. The odd Milner . . . and nobody else." She read the optician's notes on Jonathan's eye test. "No change," she said. "Lucky parents. Glasses are pricey enough at the best of times."

Trewley sighed. She ignored him, applying herself to Amanda's file as the superintendent applied his reluctant duster to that of Jonathan. "Waghorn, Paine, and Milner," she announced. "Quite a few Milner, but I think . . . Yes." She had used the tongs to remove Amanda's record card from inside the wallet and read the details. "*Poor* parents," she amended. "Little sister came in the same day—and there's a change of prescription. I imagine Mrs. Milner helped the child pick a new set of frames."

They settled into a routine. Stone powdered, taped, and studied: Trewley wrote, dusted, and silently fretted that it might all turn out to be a waste of time. The prints Stone was finding were always legitimate, if that was the word he wanted. From the three Abbotts (if there was a father, he either went elsewhere or had perfect eyesight) they moved on to Adams, Susan Mary. Waghorn and Paine. The same was true of Adams, Elizabeth Mary, and of Amwell, Jane, although the latter had several Milner prints that Stone, peeping at the card inside, confirmed as yet another result of a change in prescription and some new frames to match the lenses.

Andrews, Pandora Amabel (age six) was similarly free from particular suspicion. Even in his growing gloom the superintendent managed to feel sorry for the child, wondering aloud whether her parents were deaf or daft.

"Or deliberately obtuse," suggested Stone. "Or perhaps they just like fancy names. This must be Mother." She was working on Andrews, Mirabel Amanda of the same address. "And Grannie lives with them," she hazarded as Andrews, Prunella (aged sixty-eight) was next out of the drawer.

"Appleby, William George," said Stone, busy with her brush and sticky tape. "Date of birth—ah!"

Trewley dropped his pen and peered over her shoulder. "Ah?" he echoed. "What?"

"Waghorn," she said, "of course—and Paine—but there are others. And I don't mean smudges. Some of the others are Milner, but . . ."

"Ah," said Trewley, not daring to hope.

"Could you pass me Miss Anonymous, please?" Stone put out an unseeing hand. Trewley, without speaking, gave her what she required.

She did not thank him. She was far too preoccupied. There followed an almost unbearable silence while she gazed through the magnifying glass first at the prints she had brought with her, then at the unknown prints from the file of William George Appleby.

Unknown prints that in some places overlay the older prints of those who had a right to leave them. Unknown prints that did not belong to Mr. Paine, or Mrs. Milner, or Richard Waghorn . . .

"Yes," said Stone at last. "Yes. It's . . . possible."

"Can't you be sure?"

"The prints aren't entirely clear, sir. There's still more of the ones we know than of the unknown . . . but there's the record card to check. If our guess is right, they might be better there."

"Are they?" He hardly gave her time to examine the first photo as it slipped at last from the camera. "Well?"

She put down the magnifying glass and turned to him with a look of triumph on her face.

"Yes," said Detective Sergeant Stone.

Seventeen

"OUR DEAD BLONDE?" barked the superintendent.

"Yes," said Stone again and couldn't hide her relief. Even Trewley's face softened in a fleeting smile until she held out the photographs and, after a moment, the magnifying glass. "See for yourself if you don't believe me, sir," she invited. "Miss Anonymous, loud and clear."

The smile vanished. "I believe you," said Trewley with a scowl. Then he shrugged. "All right, let's have a look." He found it easier to compare the two sets of prints without the glass, and couldn't help resenting that Stone had guessed this would be the case. "What's so special about William George Appleby?" he said as he handed back the photographs. Before she could reply—she was already busy powdering the next wallet—he answered his own question.

"We can't tell until we've got some more," he said and put the Appleby file to one side.

"Arnold, Jeremiah," said Stone. "Gosh! I hope when I'm his age the only thing wrong with me is my eyesight."

Trewley wrote Mr. Arnold's details on the pad and in dignified silence resumed his contemplation of the William Appleby conundrum. It wasn't so much that he was getting old—he was hardly middle-aged. He was just . . . maturing. But he still didn't care to have the fact forced down his throat by a—by a chit of a girl . . .

Arnold, Primrose—Jeremiah's wife. Arrowsmith, Martin. Arundel, Lewis. Arundel, Myra. Ashburton, Arthur.

Ashley, Caroline; Ashley, Charlotte. They were sisters of a similar vintage to the Arnolds. Stone had a feeling that they were also friends, or at least acquaintances, of the Misses Clench who had reported the leaking gas and the ecdysiast bank robbers. Neither she nor Trewley cared to comment on this coincidence.

Ashley, Philip Ambrose. A different address, the same prints: Waghorn, Paine, and Milner. Ashurst, Francis . . .

"Well?" snapped Trewley as Stone tensed in the way he was coming to recognise.

She could hear him grinding his teeth as she worked. "Yes," she announced at last. "It's her." Grammar was forgotten in this second, confirmatory triumph. "Waghorn and Paine as usual, the occasional Milner—and Miss Anonymous inside and out—record card and wallet, the same as William George Appleby."

"Ah," said Trewley, the corrugated features relaxing once more into a smile. "Then we were right. And it's odds on she *is* the missing optician from Leeds."

"Y-yes," said Stone with little hesitation. "Yes, the coincidence would be too much if she weren't. But the question still is, what exactly was she looking for? What's so special about Francis Ashurst and William Appleby?"

Trewley stirred. "When you first said Francis I thought of my cousin, until you spelled it. They'll call him Frank, I dare say, but we called her Frannie. Frances. Made me think—wonder—if it might be a . . . a gender thing." With another scowl he dared his female sergeant to say too much.

"There have been other men she didn't look at," Stone said in her Devil's Advocate role. "As far as I can tell," prudence made her add. "We all make mistakes—though I'm sure I haven't—but I would say Jeremiah Arnold and Philip Ashley didn't take her fancy. And if you're right, sir, it's still a question of what makes Ashurst and Appleby so special, isn't it?"

"They don't live anywhere in particular," Trewley said, mentally reviewing his map of Allingham as he checked the addresses on the files. "Certainly not near Hobson's. Or Eye Deal or Coates, come to that."

"Two's not a fair sample, sir." Stone had her brush poised above the file for Astell, Joseph Mallord. "Third time might make it lucky."

But they were not in luck with Joseph Astell, nor with Lillian Astrupp. Catherine Aubrey and Charles of that ilk drew a similar blank. Nora Avenal was likewise unless for the purposes of investigation . . .

But with the prints from the file of Richard Avenal they had their third.

"Men, then," said Trewley. "I was right."

"Young men," amended Stone. "Youngish, anyway," she amended further. Trewley opened his mouth and then shut it again. "Appleby's what, twenty-seven?" said Stone, leaning across to look at the file. "Ashley is thirty-six, and this Avenal is twenty-eight."

"Umph." Trewley rubbed his chin and glared at the three buff cardboard pockets as if willing them to tell him what he wanted to know. "Avenal's married, I suppose," he said. "Or else this Nora's his sister. Same address."

"We can't be sure that Appleby and Ashley and Aubrey aren't married," objected Stone. "Their wives might have perfect eyesight. Or they might prefer being tested at one of the other places."

Trewley grunted again and went back to his glaring.

"Perhaps they all have beautiful blue eyes," suggested Stone after a few fruitless moments during which she had not even pulled out the next file.

"Nothing wrong with brown," muttered the superintendent. "Or even mud," he added in deference to his sergeant's chameleon hazel-grey.

"I don't think it tells us," said Stone, pulling out the record card for William Appleby. "No, it doesn't." She was about to slip the card back when Trewley shot out a hand to stop her.

"Take out the other two," he told her. "Quick."

She knew what he meant. After a few seconds' fumbling she found space on the table to spread them in line. Trewley favoured them for several seconds with one of his most ferocious scowls, and then nodded.

"Read 'em," he told her. "I can see it from here, being so much older." He couldn't resist the dig. "You'll need to pick 'em up—go on, girl. Read what they say."

Obediently she picked up the record cards one after the other, but she was puzzled. "I, um, can't speak optician, sir," she said. "I mean, I don't know what they mean—all those funny plus and minus signs. And, um, I didn't know you knew at all."

"I don't," snapped Trewley. "Nobody can make sense of 'em unless they've been trained—I thought you understood that was why we were here in the first place?"

"Well . . . yes, sir, but—"

"But if *you* can't, and you're halfway to being a doctor, then what I can't be optician language, can it?"

"Er, no sir," said Stone, once she had untangled all the "cans." She looked at the first of the three cards she held. She read out a date.

She stopped reading.

She put down the cards. "Three," she said. "Just three cards for three people—whereas some of the patients, like Jeremiah Arnold, have positively bulging folders. They've been coming here for years . . ."

"And these three characters haven't," supplied Trewley as she stopped. "Right." For the first time he was willing to say aloud what, until now, they had only dared to guess at. "So now we've a fair idea who—what—we're looking for, Stone. A bloke can change his name. He can lie about his age, within reason. He can marry, or at least shack up with some woman—but he can't change his eyesight unless he goes in for contact lenses, or some of that fancy laser-beam business that you wouldn't catch me letting anyone do, not if you paid me a million pounds."

She had picked up the cards again. "Someone between . . . twenty-five and forty," she mused aloud. She thought back some days to her idle remarks on the subject of denim jeans and the statistical details of those who wore them. "That must be a good quarter of the men on the list, sir."

"Which makes it just one eighth of the total number of patients," he replied at once. "We'll keep going to the end of the A's—no, make that to the end of the B's—and if the pattern's still the same, we can finish the alphabet doing what I reckon the chummies did. Riffle through looking for a bloke about the right age and pull him out to check how long he's been coming here—and if it's since he was a kid, we'll ignore him."

"And if there's only one card . . ."

"Ten to one her prints will be there," said Trewley with a satisfied grin; but Stone did not choose to take the bet.

They knew that it wouldn't be quite as easy as the superintendent made it sound, but now their original theory had been more or less confirmed, it gave an extra dimension to the task of powdering, printing, and photographing the files for male patients between twenty-five and forty. For safety, Stone insisted on checking those with either one or two cards. But she never found any sign that the intruders had been so thorough, and resolved to stop at the end of the B's. As a control measure she also pulled out and printed every tenth file regardless of the patient's age, sex, or marital status; but by the time they had reached Bywater, Stephen they knew they were right. They were looking—as the intruders who had abducted and killed Mr. Paine had been looking—for a man not young, but not old, who had become a patient of Hobson's Choice within the past four years.

"I've been thinking, sir." Stone paused with Cabell, Henry in mid-air. "Should we phone the station to see if they've had confirmation from Leeds that our dead blonde is the missing optician? Because if she is . . . Well, if you'd care to ring, I could be checking the end of the alphabet."

Trewley was glad of the chance to abandon his dusting. "We need to know if they found what they were looking for," he said as he dialled. "Her death *looked* like an accident, but maybe it was deliberate. If they'd found— she'd found—what they wanted, she'd be no more use to them. Those rubber gloves they didn't make her wear . . ."

He shuddered, then straightened as the phone at the other end was picked up. "Pleate? Trewley. Any news from Leeds yet about those prints?"

When at last he put down the handset he was grinning. "Anne Askew," he said. "Mrs. Ophthalmic optician. Carry on, Sergeant."

His sergeant, too, was big with news. "They found what they wanted," she told him. "There are none of her prints on the first—last—two males under Y." She didn't have to add that these two males were relative newcomers to the Hobson practice, and aged between twenty-five and forty. "Rowland Yorke and John Yates: nothing."

Trewley's instinct was to suppress his growing optimism. "We've still to find the one they wanted," he said. "And perhaps they didn't reach the end because they were interrupted by Paine. Perhaps they always meant to come back later and couldn't because the place has been swarming with bluebottles for the past week."

"Perhaps," she said rather irritably, "they found and removed the one they wanted, and we'll never know who it was. Think positive, sir. Please!"

He rumbled on the brink of an explosion for several tense moments before, with a shrug of resignation, calming down. "Carry on," he said again and picked up his pen to add Henry Cabell's details to his list.

STONE PUT DOWN her tongs, rubbed the small of her back, and stretched. "Cramp," she explained. "And my eyes are seeing things all wiggly." She blinked rapidly several times, and stretched again. "And we're only up to K," she lamented.

"As good as halfway," said Trewley. "Think positive, remember? We know we're on the right track now. I hadn't realised there were so many blokes that age around these parts needing to wear glasses."

"Or contact lenses . . . Ugh." Stone stifled a yawn. "Sorry, sir. And you were right about one thing, or at least not alone in your opinion. I haven't spotted anyone who's opted for the laser-beam treatment."

"Unless they took the file out when the patient left," said Trewley. "Damn! I wish you hadn't reminded me—"

"Think positive," she reminded him quickly. "Halfway there, and the night's still young . . . Keeldar, Shirley," she read from the next file; and Trewley wrote it down.

"Sir," said Stone, "I may be on to something."

Trewley abandoned his duster. "Yes?"

"This chap's a blank. Waghorn, Paine, one or two Milner—and not a single print from Anne Askew, though he fits the bill to perfection."

"He does indeed," said Trewley, consulting his notes. "Rowdy, Arthur John, age twenty-nine, first appointment last year—and you're sure she hasn't checked him?"

"As sure as I can be."

"Let's make doubly sure," he said after a moment. "They might just have missed him while they were looking through. Carry on until the next prospect—and if he's blank as well, we'll know we've cracked it."

Stone carried on. "Ruthyn, Dudley," she said, after the usual riffle through the drawer; but this time the superintendent did not write it down.

He watched every move she made—the gentle brushing of the powder, the careful rolling and folding of the sticky tape, the study through the glass of print after print . . .

"Double, sir," she finally announced. "She's not here."

Trewley heaved a sigh of deep and heartfelt relief. "So now we know where we are," he said. "Almost," he added with a return to his habitual caution.

"Who's the last likely candidate on your list?" enquired Stone, picking up the duster and doing the honours while her superior consulted his pad.

"Rolleston, Felix," he said, rubbing his chin. "I know that name from somewhere."

"He's a cabbie," said Stone, whose knowledge of local traffic problems was—due to the circumstances of her private life—necessarily more detailed than that of the superintendent. "Not a very good driver, by all accounts—

but he's said to be very handsome," she added. Success had made her light-headed.

"Only a fool would think they were after him for having given 'em a lift somewhere local," Trewley said. "If it was him they wanted, they came here on purpose to find him *as him*. If they wanted him as a taxi driver, there are easier ways of finding a cab than breaking into shops and attacking innocent bystanders."

She knew he hadn't meant it to sound as if she were the fool. "If I'd been looking for someone," she said slowly, "under duress—which we're assuming Anne Askew did— and if I found him, I would try to leave a clue. Extra prints on the file, tear a corner, something like that—but . . ."

"They'll have kept their eyes on her," Trewley said. "And they'll have been able to do it, too. Three of 'em in gloves, remember. One to watch the road, one to watch her, one to look through the files for likely prospects. You can bet the one watching her wouldn't have given her a chance to leave a clue."

Frowning, Stone nodded. "Yes . . . even though there's no obvious sign, Felix could well be our man," she said. "Mind you, if it had been me, I would have taken the relevant file out and lost it instead of putting it back."

"Didn't want to arouse suspicion," Trewley said. "And if poor old Paine hadn't heard something in the middle of the night and come down to be killed, it wouldn't have been aroused. An ordinary burglary, we'd have said. After a few of those designer frames Mrs. Crabtree was telling us about. They'd have killed poor Askew miles away from here— taken her back to Leeds or somewhere—and whatever happened to Felix would have no connection to anything.

"He can't be such a bad driver," he went on after further thought. "Not now. Not if the council's licenced him to run a cab—but suppose he used to be a rotten driver where he lived before. Suppose there was an accident and it was all his fault for—dammit, for refusing to wear his glasses . . ."

"Revenge," said Stone, savouring the word. "Poetic justice. They don't believe he's really turned over a new leaf—or they resent the way he's taken a driving job and think he ought to be stopped for the benefit of—"

"Hey!" Trewley's shout was accompanied by a slap of his hand that had the table rattling. "Say that again!"

"They think he ought to be stopped," she said again. "For the benefit of the general pub—"

"No, no—not that—*they resent the way he's taken a driving job*," he quoted at her, almost roaring the words. "Didn't we say the bloke who drove the getaway car for the Allshire and National business had to know the local roads like the back of his hand? So tell me who knows the roads better than a taxi driver!"

Eighteen

HE GAVE HER no time to tell him he was right. He snatched up the writing pad from the table and waved it under her nose. "See where he lives!" he demanded.

Again he gave her no time to speak, although she would have liked to tell him she couldn't possibly see the address because it was dancing up and down in front of her eyes. "I know where this is," he said in triumph. "Don't you? It's one of those flats above the shops on the other side of the market square from the Allshire and National Bank!"

He dropped the pad back on the table and lumbered to his feet. "We're going round there," he said. "Now. We want the answers to a hell of a lot of questions, Stone."

"Yes, sir," replied the sergeant. "Will we be coming back, or should I pack everything away and take it with me?"

"Ah." Trewley stopped in mid-stride. "Coming back. We promised Mrs. Milner we'd tidy up behind us, didn't we?" He caught her eye. "You did, at any rate," he amended.

"In the interests of public relations," she said sternly, and began to load her equipment into the bag while he stumped up and down the shop, muttering, from the front door to the filing cabinet and back.

His conscience made him flick the duster a few times as she went on packing, but even in the interests of public relations she was not prepared to push him too far when a case seemed so near its conclusion. She took one last look around the empty shop as, with everything done, they finally reached the door. "Creepy, isn't it?" she said. "Could be someone's worst nightmare—all those empty frames staring like horrible blank, dead faces. Ugh."

"Stop philosophising and come on," commanded Trewley; and she switched off the lights and locked the door.

"We'll see our taxi driver first," said Trewley as they headed for the car. "It's on the way to Mrs. Milner's. We can drop the keys off later—although how much later is going to depend on what we learn from Rolleston." His voice darkened. "And where we learn it." If they had to take the man to the station for questioning, it could end up being a long night.

Hobson's Choice was at the end of a street not far from the market square, and it did not take them long to reach Felix Rolleston's flat. "Someone's home," Trewley said as they climbed out of the car. "Any fool knows to leave a light on in the hall, but when it's in the bathroom you can be pretty sure they haven't gone out for the evening."

Stone glanced at her watch. "He could be getting ready to go out," she said. "Best bib and tucker and dinner for two—or clean white shirt for a fussy client he's driving on a business trip—"

"He'll have to talk to us before he goes," growled Trewley; and she subsided.

They had to ring the doorbell twice before the intercom clicked into life. "Who is it?" asked a man with a strong, but not uneducated, local accent.

"This is the police," said Trewley. "Superintendent Trewley, Allingham CID. Is that Mr. Rolleston?"

"Police?" The accent hesitated. It sounded more than usually wary. "Anyone can say that. How do I know?"

"Stone, get ready to nip round the front and shove a light on the roof," Trewley said quietly. In a louder voice he said, "Mr. Rolleston? If you'd care to take a look out of your front window you'll see my sergeant standing by the car. Would you like her to switch on the flashing blues and let all the neighbours know you've got visitors?"

"No," said the local accent, investing the word with deep dismay. "No, don't—I'll come down—wait there!"

"He might make a run for it," said Trewley. "There's an emergency exit the other end of the block."

"I'm keeping my eyes peeled, sir," said Stone, balanced on the balls of her feet ready to run.

The precaution seemed to have been in vain. The sound of feet clattering down concrete steps and along a passage drew gradually closer until, with a bang, a heavy bolt slid across the door. There came the clink of a safety chain, the scrape of a turned handle, and a suspicious, bespectacled eye peered out of the six-inch gap between the edge of the door and its jamb.

"Mr. Rolleston?"

"Oh, blimey." Trewley had moved into the light that filtered out through the six-inch gap, holding his identity card for the man to have a proper view. The sight did not appear to have cheered him. "Oh, blimey," said the man for a second time. "Yes, well—hang on. You can come in."

"He doesn't sound too happy, sir," whispered Stone as the door shut in their faces for Rolleston—if, indeed, it was he—to release the safety chain.

"Good," muttered Trewley. "Catch 'em off balance, and they spill the beans faster. That's the way I like it—ah. Good evening, sir. Mr. Felix Rolleston?"

"Yes," admitted that gentleman, with obvious reluctance. "Look, is this going to take long?"

"That all depends." Trewley was projecting his Dogged Determination persona, the one that would go without sleep to ascertain the truth. "May we come in?"

Felix Rolleston gazed at Superintendent Trewley intently for a moment or two and then sighed. Mr. Rolleston's shoulders drooped, his face grew pale, and his quiet good looks seemed to wither as in their turn the detectives gazed at him. Without a word he turned on his heel and began to walk along the passage to the stairs. Trewley and Stone, the latter pausing to close the outside door, walked after him.

The three clattered in single file up the stairs. The air was chilly as they walked along the tiled passage to Rolleston's flat. He had left the door ajar.

"Come in," he said. Trewley and Stone had had heartier

welcomes in their time. They went in. Rolleston lurked by
the door to close it after them. "Go through," he said, and
nodded at what must be—was—the dining room. The flat
was laid out along the same plan as the Paine flat over
Hobson's Choice.

"So what seems to be the trouble?" Mr. Rolleston hovered
for a moment in the doorway, then drifted into the room and
stood with his back against the wall. His eyes darted from
Trewley's face to Stone's, unable now to meet the gaze of
either detective for more than an instant. He took off his
glasses and wiped the back of his hand across his brow.

"May we sit down?" Trewley had signalled to Stone to
leave her notebook in her pocket for the moment. There was
something nagging at the back of his mind that made him
less sure of himself than he'd been at first.

"Please yourselves." Mr. Rolleston replaced his glasses
and, with a sigh, took a chair at the dining-room table. The
legs scraped on the floor, setting Stone's teeth on edge.

"We apologise for bothering you when you're obviously
busy," Trewley said, trying to sound as if he meant it.

"It's your job," said Mr. Rolleston with another sigh.

"Whereas your job," said Trewley, "is driving cars, isn't
it?"

Behind his lenses the eyes of Mr. Rolleston glinted like
those of a wild creature in a trap. He flushed and looked
away. "Yes," he admitted in a mumble. He did not sound
happy about the admission.

"Been driving long?" enquired Trewley.

Once more Mr. Rolleston took off his glasses and mopped
his brow. "Near enough three years," he said, wriggling on
his chair as he caught the quick exchange of glances
between Trewley and Stone.

"What did you do before?" Trewley was leading his way
gently to the big question.

Rolleston licked his lips. "Storeman," he said, and sighed
again. His eyes darted once about the room as if impressing
every last detail on his memory, and then he ducked his
head. "Below," he said, and could not meet the superintendent's gaze.

The gaze was one of bewilderment. "Below?" echoed Trewley, blinking at him.

"You mean," broke in Stone before her superior could betray his confusion, "in the shop downstairs?"

"That's right." Mr. Rolleston lifted his head to reveal an expression of mingled surprise that she needed to ask, and guilt. "That's why you're here, isn't it? I thought I c-couldn't get away with it forever—but it's a bit thick to send you lot round without even a solicitor's letter."

The interview was somehow going in a different direction from the one he'd expected, but with those final words Trewley felt on safe ground once more. "A solicitor?" he said. "You mean you'd prefer not to make a statement unless you've taken legal advice? We can arrange that easily enough once we're at the station, Mr. Rolleston."

Felix Rolleston's eyes widened. "C-can't you just give me time to—to find another place and save yourselves the trouble of taking me to court? My girlfriend—"

"Court?" It was all getting too much for Trewley. "We haven't even charged you yet. And as for—"

"Mr. Rolleston!" It was so rare for Stone to interrupt her superior in mid-interrogation that he could only gape at her as she pressed on: "Mr. Rolleston, how long were you a storeman before you became a cabbie?"

Rolleston's shoulders hunched. "Eight years," he said. "One extra. Thought I'd g-got rights after seven, see?"

"I see," said Stone, who did.

Trewley, who didn't, held his peace. There were times when he knew he had to trust her. Stone, too, having said that she saw, said no more: Often silence brought quicker results than a battery of questions.

"Nice little flat," said Felix Rolleston in a wistful voice. "Goes—went—with the job, see? But when I handed in my notice there wasn't anyone else to take it on, being as it suits a single bloke best and the others were all family men. That's why I waited until all my mates was married and I knew they didn't plan to take on anyone else." Yet again he removed his glasses and mopped his brow as he cast a melancholy eye about the dining room. "Thought I was safe," he said sadly. "But it—it won't count against me, will it? My taxi licence, I mean. I can't pay the back rent—not a lump sum, if that's what they're asking—but I've kept this place in good nick, and they can't say I haven't. Paint, paper, done the plumbing myself . . . But I don't want to go . . . to go to p-prison. If it comes to c-court I—"

He choked himself to a halt. His fingers played with the earpieces of his spectacles, opening and closing them, his gaze fastened on them so that he would not have to look his visitors in the face.

Trewley was lost for words. Stone, somewhat breathless, was not. "How long have you worn glasses, Mr. Rolleston?" she asked gently.

"Since a kid," he said. "Hate them."

"And where do you have your eyes tested?" was her next question. Trewley, his nagging doubt more certain now, did not try to take the conversation over.

"Coates, as a rule—no, I tell a lie." Mr. Rolleston shook on his chair as if the penalties for perjury and claiming squatter's rights were equally severe. "H-hobson, the last time," he said, trying to steady his voice. "But there's nobody can say I'm not fit to drive, because it's not true. With my specs I can see as well as anyone. I'm as safe on the road as you yourself—and if I ain't so keen on driving at night, well, that's nobody's business but mine." As his agitation increased, his accent grew stronger. "At least," he protested, "I've the sense to know I'm not so good in the dark, and I take precautions. If they're so wicked as to lose me my licence on account of my eyes, I—"

"No!" cried Stone. "Sir," she added. "This is nothing to do with the shop downstairs, or your flat," she went on. "They haven't breathed a word to us, honestly—and in any case it would be a civil matter, dealt with through solicitors and so on, the way you thought. We're just . . . following up a lead on something else. All we need to know is how long you've been having your eyes tested in Allingham, when you changed from Coates to Hobson, and whether you went to anyone else first."

"And *why* you changed," put in Trewley, who felt he

ought to make his presence felt and couldn't think of anything else to ask.

Mr. Rolleston looked puzzled. "Since I was a kid," he said. "I told you." He was so puzzled that he forgot to be nervous, though his accent remained strong. "My mum it was took me to Coates," he said. "Six or seven, I was when I started to wear the things, and Coates being in the town centre was handy, which is why she still goes there. But I fancied a change when they went on the computer and never sent me a reminder card, when I was told to have them checked every year on account of my—my astigmatic axis keeps changing. If I'm not regular with my prescriptions I get these awful headaches, see. And when the girl just giggled at me and said they must have forgotten, I thought I'd try someone who looked after you a bit better than stick you in a computer and forget all about you."

Whoever had broken into Eye Deal had not found what they were looking for; they had moved on to Hobson's Choice, to look there; they did not appear to have honoured Coates with their attentions. Perhaps the Rolleston file—his address, his name—had been the one they wanted.

Perhaps not.

As Rolleston—who must know they could check this— had been a Coates client until comparatively recently, if those who were looking for him had gone there first and found him at once, would they still have needed to break into the other two opticians? Might Paine—perhaps even Askew—not have been killed?

Or had there been some other reason for the break-ins and murders than the search for Felix Rolleston's name and address? There was the matter of the Allshire and National robbery to bear in mind . . .

"Where," asked Trewley, "were you last Friday afternoon between three and four, sir?"

A rueful, lopsided grin set Mr. Rolleston's eyes twinkling behind the spectacles he had long since replaced on his nose. The grin made him look almost as handsome as Stone's little joke had suggested. "In the repair shop," he said. "Me and half the town, I should think, seeing it took

forever for the tow trucks to arrive and we all went at once."
Gaining confidence, he chuckled. "My insurance couldn't
believe me," he enlarged, "when I told 'em there I was
minding my own business and this ruddy great lorry,
begging your pardon, full of bananas caught fire right in
front of me and almost had my eyebrows off, never mind the
paint, and— Was it something I said?" he broke off to add,
as Trewley emitted a groan and Stone, despite herself,
giggled. "But I shouldn't have thought you lot would need
telling," went on Mr. Rolleston with another grin. "Talk
about red-hot. Your Traffic lad's pen must've been hotter
than that lorry with all the details he was having to write
down and everyone yelling at him at once . . ."

"I HAD MY doubts as soon as I heard him speak," said
Trewley as they walked back to the car. His hands were
thrust deep in his trouser pockets, and he was not a happy
man.

"For all we knew he could have moved away from home
for a while and come back again," said the loyal Stone.
"Come back after—um—whatever incident it might have
been that had the chummies in hot pursuit."

"Except that he says they aren't," came her companion's
glum reminder. "Whoever is after whoever else, for whatever reason, with Rolleston out of the frame we've no more
chance than we had before of working out what the hell's
going on. We'll talk to the garage, of course—but he wasn't
lying. He's a regular customer. They won't forget a day like
that any more than we can."

"Unlike the Coates' computer," murmured Stone, herself
doing a spot of pocket-delving in search of the car keys. "It
only goes to prove how true it is: Garbage in, garbage out.
The human element can never be—"

"Coates!" cried Trewley. Stone dropped the keys. "The
computer!" he shouted. "That's why they'll have tried the
smaller places first—even I know every blasted computer
system is different—but the reminders! Stone, listen." He
wagged a finger under her startled nose as she straightened
from retrieving the keys. "You're one of the lucky ones," he

said, and for once it wasn't an accusation. "You don't wear glasses."

"Well, not yet," she admitted cautiously. "Though I imagine that in time—"

"But you go to the dentist, don't you? Of course you do," he answered on her behalf. "They send you a reminder card—YOUR NEXT CHECK-UP IS OVERDUE—and don't tell me you don't need reminders, because I know you don't. I'm just making the point, dammit, that most people aren't nearly as well organised."

"Er—possibly not," she conceded with a frown.

"I'm not," he told her. "My wife does the reminding, but with five of us she can't always keep track, and they still send a card to be on the safe side."

"Oh," said Stone, who was starting to understand. "You mean if we go back to Hobson's now . . ."

"Now," said Trewley, and he made it a command.

ONCE THEY WERE inside the shop he became noticeably less sanguine. "Fifty to one they'll have thought of it, too," he muttered as he surveyed the scene in front of him.

"They didn't take the appointments diary." With a brisk forefinger Stone tapped the thick red ledger that had pride of place in the middle of the main desk.

"It could have been last year," said Trewley, determined to look on the black side.

"Remember Forensic's list of contents?" Determination could work both ways. Stone was not going to allow a good idea to go to waste before it had even been tested. "They said," she reminded him, "there are ledgers a mile high in the storage area. You can bet there's a decade of diaries out there, when we need only three years, four at most—but we'll try the current system first, I think."

"Well, go ahead," he said. "Anything's worth a try. Though he's probably moved somewhere else by now."

Stone swallowed an exasperated sigh. "He's sure to have done," she agreed. If you couldn't beat him, join him in his gloom. "But this looks promising—oh, no, it's a list of suppliers." She dropped the lid on the blue plastic card-index box and opened another. "It's a pity," she said severely, "that colour coding is more fashionable than plain printed labels. How an outsider can be expected to— Ah."

Trewley looked at her, but said nothing. "Well, we're getting warmer," she told him as he was clearly bent on continued gloom. "This is for patients who have to collect new prescriptions. He might be in here—but we can't be certain. Third time lucky?"

She lifted the lid of the largest box. "Ah," she said once again, and in such a tone that Trewley ventured to brighten. "This looks . . . this is it, sir."

"Ah," echoed Trewley, edging nearer. "Well?"

She thrust the box at him. "You call them out while I check the files," she said. "Sir," she added, in case she had sounded too peremptory. He uttered an irritated snort and waved her away to the filing cabinet over which she had already laboured so long . . .

But it should not take so long on this occasion. "Start with Rolleston?" she suggested. "He's the last one we can be sure about."

"Rolleston," agreed Trewley as he took index cards A to Q inclusive in a mighty grip and removed them, and what they indexed, from the box and dumped them on the table. "Clear the way," he explained as Stone—who had a healthy respect for paperwork even if, like most people, she avoided it as much as possible—winced. "Carry on," he commanded; and she pulled open the relevant drawer.

─── Nineteen ───

"Rolliver, James," said Trewley, ignoring the cards for all those of the feminine persuasion. Stone had already reminded him that Hilary, Evelyn, Leslie and Robin should be given the benefit of the doubt. "Rolliver, James."

"He's here," replied Stone.

There followed some rustling sounds. "Romaine, Daniel," said Trewley at last.

"Yes," said Stone.

Further rustling. Ronder, Frederick: He was there, as was Rook, Thomas. Rooney, Andrew. Roothing, Robert Albert. Rose, Timothy. Ross, Paul . . .

"No," said Stone, who had stiffened at the name.

Trewley, the card in his hand, stared at her. "Stone," he said slowly. Stone stared back at him in silence.

"Check they haven't misfiled it," he urged, his excitement growing. He was willing to bet that they hadn't.

"They haven't," reported Stone after what seemed an interminable wait. "Sir . . ."

"Who's next?" enquired Trewley, wanting to be sure. "Is it Rossiter, James?"

Stone had to force herself to consult the files again. "He's here," she said, barely containing her glee.

The superintendent rose majestically to his feet. "We'll go round there now," he said. "The address is the same— look." He held out the reminder card for Paul Ross, but she paid it no attention. It might be a coincidence, but she somehow didn't think so. This time, she thought, he was right. Paul Ross . . .

"Didn't I say," he said as once more they hurried from Hobson's Choice in pursuit of a clue, "that it was all to do with the Allshire and National business?"

"You did, sir."

"It all adds up, Stone." He watched her lock the door of the shop behind them. "He was a witness to the robbery—injured, no less. He comes out of hospital and buys every last security device Bert Gadgett has on the shelf. He was worried they'd find him, Stone."

"Yes, sir," she said again as she pattered in his wake to the car. "I wonder how they learned where he lived?"

He stopped in his tracks to curse her stupidity. "What the hell d'you think we've just spent half the night doing, Detective Sergeant Stone?"

"Going through the optician's records," she replied at once. "Sorry, sir, I phrased it badly." She was unlocking the car as she spoke. "What I meant was, I wonder how they knew to come looking for him in Allingham. I mean, charming place, county town and all that, but it hardly leaps to the eye as an immediate choice for a—for a hideout, sir."

"That depends," said the superintendent sagely, "on who is doing the hiding. And who they're hiding from."

They drove without further exchange of words to the home of Paul Ross. Stone did not even suggest using the radio to advise the station of their movements: There was too much tension in the air already that evening. Night. She had been startled when, on checking her watch, she saw that it was half-past nine.

"Three years," she said suddenly as she pulled the car into the kerb. "That's how long his neighbour with the lawn mower—the one who was complaining about the do-it-yourself noises—told us Ross had been living here," she enlarged as Trewley demanded to know what she was talking about. "Doesn't that fit in beautifully with our optician findings?"

"Let's hope," said Trewley, "we find Ross."

Neither said anything more as they hurried up the path towards the darkened house. The moon was fitful with scudding cloud, but in the light from a nearby streetlamp they could see that the curtains hung open at the fastened windows. The only sign of movement was that of stray leaves and branches disturbed by a faint breeze, reflected in the still and silent glass.

"No empties," said Trewley, glaring at the front step. "Most people have put 'em out by this time of night."

"He probably buys his milk at the supermarket," said Stone. "Or he's cancelled it because he's gone away."

"He's done a bunk," said Trewley.

"Round the back?" offered Stone.

"Both of us," he decreed, and they went together.

While the front path was paved, the side path around the house was gravel. "Guilty conscience," said Trewley, thankful there was enough moonlight, despite the clouds, to show the way in safety.

"He'll hear us coming," said Stone, "and phone the station. If Sergeant Pleate sends a patrol car, we'll never live it down."

Trewley did not remind her that it had already been decided the owner of the house was not at home to hear them.

As they turned the last corner, a shrill piping scream from above made Stone utter a quick cry.

"What's wrong?" Trewley snapped.

"Sorry, sir—a bat." Eyesight wasn't the only faculty that could, with age, deteriorate. Then she stopped again. "Sir," she said, and pointed.

His gaze followed her pointing finger. Where the gravel ended, paving stones formed a patio area at the back of the house; the flickering moonlight made cold, irregular patterns of far more than diamond brilliance.

"Broken glass," breathed Stone. "He's had burglars . . ."

"And now he's got us." Trewley stepped grimly over the shining shards to the back door. He tried the handle. It turned but did not open. "Locked from inside," he said.

"You could boost me through the window, sir." Stone had

checked that it wasn't too far from the ground. "I don't think I can pull myself up on my own, but if you could make a back, or if I stepped on your hands—"

"Let's try the doorbell first." Trewley was not going to send his sergeant into the unknown when he couldn't go with her. "We'll go back to the front," he said. "Maybe he just goes to bed early. We'll wake him up to ask." He said nothing about the broken window.

Stone pointedly said nothing about anything.

They could hear the ding-dong chime of the bell through the door as they pressed the button. "He's got to be deaf to miss that," muttered Trewley. In silence he counted to thirty and pressed the button again.

"He's done a bunk," he said after another half-minute.

"We could check the garage," suggested Stone. "Or maybe we couldn't," she added as they reached the metal up-and-over door of the brick edifice built on the side of the house. "Lost Property cupboards, yes. That sort of lock— sorry, sir, no. My penknife's not that good."

"We'll try the bell again," he said. "If there's still no answer, we'll radio for Benson or one of the others—"

"Sir!" protested Stone. "That—that's sexism. You'd make Benson hop in that broken window as soon as look at it, you know you would. If I promise to unlock the door the very first thing . . . We don't want the others to share the fun, do we? Especially," added the wily daughter of Eve, "as we're not entirely sure we're on the right track. Think of what Sergeant Pleate would have to say . . ."

She left the thought unfinished; and Trewley, tempted, fell. "First thing you find the key and open that door," he told her as she led the way back around the house. "You let me in straight away or I yell bloody blue murder and rouse the neighbourhood, Stone. I mean it."

"I promise, sir," she said. She meant it, too.

For form's sake they thumped and knocked on the kitchen door a few times before Stone took off her jacket and threw it up to the window to catch on the broken glass. Trewley, grunting, braced himself with his flank against the wall and his hands clasped low in front of him. Stone politely dusted off her shoes, put her hands on his shoulders, and set her right foot in his hands. He emitted a grunt as he threw her upwards . . . and with a few frantic scrabbles she was off his hands and halfway into the house.

"Ooof!" She was wriggling and twisting, trying to turn so that when she dropped she would fall on her feet. Agility was only one of the many benefits of a judo black belt. The listening superintendent heard her gasp again and saw her disappear into the darkness from which a loud thud announced that she had landed safely.

"Stone!" he called, but there was no need for the reminder. Even as he spoke there came a rattle at the door, and it swung open.

"Good evening, sir. Nice to see you. Just hang on while I find the light switch," said his hostess, leaving him on the step for a fifteen-second spell while she groped her way across to the kitchen door.

With a click, the light came on. Both detectives blinked at the contrast with the cloudy moonlit night outside.

"Well, let's get on with it," said Trewley.

As Stone was already beside the door and he wasn't, she was the first to move into the hall, taking a few steps along the yellow corridor of outflung electric brightness interrupted by Trewley's shadowy, shadowing bulk. "We need another light switch," she muttered—and then stopped.

"Sir," she said, putting out a warning hand.

He stopped. His eyes were still adjusting to the light and darkness contrast: hers were younger. She pushed him even farther to the side; the yellow corridor widened. "Sir," she whispered as she stared ahead. "I think . . ."

Now he could see what she could see. "Don't move," he told her. "Back away, like me. There *must* be a switch at the kitchen end somewhere. Find it."

Even at such a moment they did not forget to make their cautious retreat as close to the walls as possible. To walk down the middle of the floor was to destroy whatever traces might have been left by those who had walked there before them . . . perhaps by the still and silent figure illuminated in the kitchen light at the foot of the stairs at the far end of the hall.

"Found it," grunted Trewley. "Let's have your knife, Stone." She opened and handed it to him, blade first; he took it, reversed it, and with the tip of the blade pressed the light switch down.

They blinked in the sudden light, then stared.

There was a pregnant pause.

"Your feminist instincts won't object if I radio for Benson now, will they?" said Trewley.

"Not to mention the others," said Stone.

The said nothing more for a moment as they continued to survey the scene. The carpet along the hall, scuffed and torn in places, was in other places stained with ominously sticky red-brown smears they must take even greater pains to avoid. The sprawling figure at the foot of the staircase was that of a man, crumpled against the newel post.

Step by cautious step the two detectives drew closer. The man's one visible hand and arm, groping up the stairs with his left sleeve rucked around his elbow—Stone's quick eye spotted the gleam of a cuff button not far away—were white. His face was strangely piebald.

"Bruises," said Stone.

"Post mortem lividity," said Trewley.

They moved closer still. "Bloodstains up the stairs," said Trewley and heard his sergeant shiver. "Question is," he went on quickly, "did they fight in the bedroom and our friend here make it as far as this, or . . ."

"Or," supplied Stone, rallying, "did someone else go up there afterwards?"

"Only one way to find out," said Trewley. He hesitated. "You can go and radio now for Benson, if you like."

"I don't, thanks." Stone managed a chuckle as she began to follow him up the side of the stairs. "Apart from anything else, sir, suppose he's lying in wait somewhere? You haven't given me my knife back yet."

As Stone followed Trewley, so Trewley followed the gory trail, which grew more gory as he climbed. Some of the red-brown marks were those of fingers, not of shoes

with bloodied soles. He wished he had been firmer with his
sergeant, but it was too late now. He reached the top of the
stairs and turned to the left. A rust-coloured handprint and a
rip in the wallpaper showed where the unknown bleeder had
tripped and fallen but had dragged himself—herself?—up
again to stagger on.

On the threshold of what looked like the main bedroom,
he hesitated once more. "This could be a nasty one," he
warned.

"If he's still there," said Stone bravely. "But if he's
already got away, all we'll see is . . . is an advertisement
for biological washing powder."

"Thought you didn't hold with that stuff," Trewley said as
he leaned forward to look into the room.

"I don't," said Stone. "To use all those enzymes when a
good soaking in cold water . . ." She saw the superintendent stiffen. "Is there—anyone—there?" she asked.

She saw him nod.

THEY WERE BACK in their office after a long, grisly night.
Stone had refused to go home to bed unless her superior did
the same, and he refused to abandon his post until they had
received an answer to the faxes they had sent to the North
of England force. Tea and biscuits—yesterday's canteen
buns were stale, and today's weren't ready yet—kept the
pair going as they stifled their yawns and waited.

"I wonder," said Stone as she prepared to dunk the third
chocolate digestive in her tea, "whether the hotel will try to
sue us for payment of the outstanding bill. If Leeds don't
come up with an identity, we'll be the closest he's got to a
next of kin, won't we?"

"Don't." As Trewley shuddered, Stone giggled; and he
was glad to hear her. His sergeant had been unnaturally pale
and subdued during the preliminary stages of the recent
investigation. "That woman," he said, and shuddered again.

"Coppering is a tough job, sir. That's what you always
say. And when it's a matter of—of official obligation,
public relations . . ."

"Don't," he begged for the second time, but with a great

deal more fervour than the first. "I'll . . . send you," he threatened, groping for his handkerchief to mop his brow. "All girls together, Sergeant Stone. You'll enjoy that."

"No I won't." She licked chocolate from her fingers in a manner she felt sure the prim self-control of the dreaded hotel receptionist would never permit. "Let's think positive, sir," she went on. "Sooner or later someone, somewhere, is bound to notice that Leggett is missing—"

"*If* that was his name, which I very much doubt," Trewley grumbled. "The bloke obviously came here looking for Ross, and was quite happy to break into his house to duff him up—or worse, as we know. If you're planning that sort of caper you don't use your own name, Stone. That's why he paid the deposit in cash, remember?"

"I wonder who the other two were." Stone hesitated over a fourth biscuit, but decided in the end that a fresh mug of tea would help it down. "How about a refill?" she offered as she pushed back her chair. "I'll detour via the fax machine in case there's any news."

When she came back—rattling the handle of the office door so the superintendent had a chance to wake up—she was smiling. In her hand, under the tray, she held a curling sheet of paper. "News," she announced as she dropped her trophy on Trewley's desk and then lowered the tray to rest beside it. "Hot from the press—but I know you're going to moan about coincidence again," she added as she took the visitors' chair and raised her mug to her lips. Over the rim she watched Trewley's face as, peering through his spectacles, he perused what had been scrawled in electronic letters on the sheet of still warm paper.

He came to the end, caught her eye, and calmly read the fax again. "Umph," was all he said, but he said it with considerable force.

"Coincidence, or what?" crowed his sergeant, pushing the packet of biscuits across for him to help himself. With the news he'd just received he needed all the blood-sugar boosting he could get. "To be involved in one bank hold-up might be regarded as—as malpractice. To be involved in two . . ."

"Unlucky," was the superintendent's only comment as he read the fax for a third time. "Yes . . ."

Stone hopped up from her chair to fetch a pad and pencil from her desk. "Let's see," she said, settling herself comfortably. "Paul Ross was really Peter Russell, and what he didn't know about robbing banks was nobody's business."

"Honour among thieves," snorted Trewley, who had taken off his glasses and was stabbing at the blotter with an earpiece. "Huh!"

"Quite so, sir." Stone doodled a skull-and-crossbones beside the Ross-Russell entry on the pad. "He and his, um, former associates pull off a really big and successful job, and he skips with the lot, changes his name, and ends up in Allingham—we still don't know why."

"Why not?" retorted Trewley, Allshire born and bred.

"Why not indeed," said Stone. She'd had longer than he to think about it, and knew it wasn't as important as other aspects of the case. "The rest of the gang think his wife was in on the skipping, and they give her a really hard time until she somehow convinces them she wasn't."

"Sheri," said Trewley, snorting again. "What a name."

"Probably christened Shirley," suggested Stone. "They say a change is as good as a rest."

"Umph." The superintendent glared at her. "There's a hell of a lot of name-changing going on around here."

"Coincidence, sir." Stone was firm on this point. "And necessary, of course," she added. "Peter Russell could change his identity to Paul Ross—but he couldn't change his eyesight."

"Which is what we said all along," said Trewley. "Laser beams and contact lenses don't suit everyone, especially if they're the cowardly blasted wimps too many of the big-talk crooks who hide behind guns turn out to be. No wonder he looked in such a state when he was on the receiving end, for once!"

"But he *was* unlucky," Stone said, echoing the superintendent's own opinion. "To have that video crew in town take a close-up of him, in his specs, coming out of the bank—and shown on prime-time television—you couldn't expect that sort of thing to happen in a score of centuries. Short of leaving the country he must have thought he was safe after three years. He's not—he wasn't—the sort to go in for plastic surgery . . ."

"Painful," said Trewley. "And it costs. He got away with a lot, but not that much as a long-term prospect. He wanted security. Invest the loot, live on the interest, take a job to keep the income ticking over . . ."

"As soon as he was seen on television he was on borrowed time," said Stone. "Even with half the gang in prison for, um, non-related incidents, there was still Sheri— who was innocent of anything except complicity—and her brother and the man Lester, who was our friend Leggett from the upstairs bedroom. They were all hell-bent on revenge for one reason or another. They descended on Allingham to find out what they could. Sheri tried to pump E. M. Forster—"

"Ha!" scoffed Trewley. "That'll be the day."

"Well, yes, but she wasn't to know the man had a liver like—like I don't know what, sir." Stone shook her head for the reporter's folly, and then grinned. "He certainly bounced out of hospital a lot faster than most other people would do in similar circumstances . . ."

"To find his place had been turned over by Sheri and her pals looking for some clue about where Paul Ross lived," Trewley said. "If anyone knew anything about the people who'd been caught up in the bank robbery, it had to be the bloke who made the headline in the local paper. Trouble was, they had no idea what their long-lost chum was calling himself in this nice new life he'd made at their expense. So they worked out between them that the only way of tracing him would be through his glasses. They go back up north—his wife remembers where he used to have his eyes tested—they kidnap the poor woman who dealt with him last, the one who can work out how his prescription might change over the years he's been away, and they start breaking into one optician's after the other, looking for a bloke about the right age with the right sort of eyesight."

"This is where we have to speculate," said Stone, as if

that wasn't what they'd been doing until then. "They find a likely prospect in the Hobson files, and Sheri—who's dyed her hair, as Forster told us—goes with Leggett-Lester to see who lives at the address on the card. She probably went to the front door pretending to be an Avon lady or something. He'd be distracted—confused—long enough to allow Leggett time to break in at the back . . ."

"Well spotted about the fresh putty," Trewley said. He would have expected no less of her, but a compliment once in a while should do her no lasting harm.

"I wanted to see what kind of a state my jacket would be in when Forensic let me have it back," said Stone. "They'd have spotted it, too, I'm sure."

"Make a note," said Trewley, "to check whether Ross or whatever we're calling him recently bought a pane of glass from Bert Gadgett. It's where he got the window locks after he'd seen that he might be in danger—I suppose everyone told him when he went back to work how they'd recognised him on the telly. He was quick enough to work out that if his friends could do it, so could his enemies . . ."

"I suppose he killed them both," said Stone after some minutes had elapsed. "Sheri and Leggett, I mean. They would surely have gone back to the hotel if they'd been able—if they'd been still alive—to tell Black, I mean Brown, Sheri's brother, that they'd found him. Or not, if they hadn't." She made a face. "The bodies can't be far away, that's one thing. Ross was desperate, yes, but he was pretty badly damaged *before* brother Brown came to find out what had gone wrong and left that poor optician tied up and gagged in the hotel for Mrs. Boyle to trip over . . ."

"Brown broke into what he knew, because they hadn't come back, must be the right address," said Trewley, picking up the thread as she fell silent again. "Ross was waiting for him." He rubbed his chin in thought. "That Sunday we went round for a chat and he wasn't home . . . I wonder if he'd gone off looking for the gun in London or somewhere nice and anonymous like that. It would fit."

"I hope it was quick however he killed them," Stone said.

knowing from the evidence of Paul Ross's bruises that it had probably been far from quick.

"Umph," said Trewley, who knew it, too. "Brown hadn't been in the wars the way Ross had," he went on. "It was a tough fight—and Ross must have been killed before he could tell Brown what had happened to his sister and Leggett. He just about dragged himself upstairs to see if they were in one of the bedrooms . . ."

"And that," said Stone, "was that."

"Poor old Paine," said Trewley, who by now had dug a sizeable hole in his blotter and was scraping shreds of pink paper into dusty heaps with his spectacles. "He was just in the wrong place at the wrong time—and I don't mean the Allshire and National hold-up. Which we've still got on the books, Sergeant, so don't think we can relax just yet."

"I wasn't going to, sir."

"No," said Trewley in an absent tone of voice. "That was another bit of bad luck—but at least I feel sorry for him. You can't ask me to feel the same way about Ross—or his wife—or their so-called friends."

For a moment or two Stone did not reply. "You mean," she said at last, "coincidence, sir." Trewley looked at her. "As well as bad luck," she added. "Poor Mr. Paine," she enlarged as he continued to look.

He yawned and stretched. "We can tidy up the rest of it tomorrow," he said. "Let's go home."

"You mean," she ventured to correct him for a second time, "today, sir. Look at the clock."

"Ugh," said Trewley. "Today, then." He yawned again.

"And tomorrow," he quoted, "is another day. So change the calendar, will you, there's a good girl?"

She tore off yesterday's sheet for the day-to-day pad on the corner of his desk. "Another month," she corrected him yet again with a twinkle in her eye.

"Good grief," Trewley, replacing his glasses to see for himself, chuckled. "April the first—you're not joking, Sergeant. Another month . . . And that makes me one up on my wife." He snatched off his spectacles and waved them in Stone's direction. "Which I must say makes a change, for once." He grinned. "When I go home for breakfast I can tell her that I've remembered before she does that April's the month I'm due at the optician's for a check-up . . ."

SARAH J. MASON

Sarah J(ill) Mason was born in England (Bishop's Stortford) and went to university in Scotland (St. Andrews). She then lived for a year in New Zealand (Rotorua) before returning to settle only twelve miles from where she started. She now lives about twenty miles outside London with a tame welding engineer husband and two (reasonably) tame Schipperke dogs. Her first (non-series) mystery, *Let's Talk of Wills*, was published in the United States in 1986.

Seeing is Deceiving is her sixth title featuring Trewley and Stone. Under the pseudonym Hamilton Crane, she has written twelve "Miss Seeton" books in the series created by the late Heron Carvic.